Also by William H. Armstrong

SOUNDER

Awarded the 1970 Newbery Medal

SOUR LAND

SOUR LAND

WILLIAM H. ARMSTRONG

SCHOLASTIC INC.
New York Toronto London Auckland Sydney

ISBN 0-590-47097-3

Copyright © 1971 by William H. Armstrong. All rights reserved. Published by Scholastic Inc., 730 Broadway, New York, NY 10003, by arrangement with HarperCollins Children's Books, a division of HarperCollins Publishers.

12 11 10 9 8 7 6 5 4 3 2   3 4 5 6 7 8/9

Printed in the U.S.A.   40

First Scholastic printing, October 1993

"A good man is immune to misfortune, for whatever evil befalls him leaves him still his own soul."

MARCUS AURELIUS

SOUR LAND

1

"WHY is one kind of graveyard called a cemetery and the other a burying ground?" David Stone asked his father as they paused at a point where a high wire fence ran at right angles down the hill from Anson Stone's pasture fence.

"They bury Negroes in one and us in the other," Jonathan Stone interrupted before his father could answer.

"But if they're both graveyards, why is one so messy and the other so neat?" the third child asked. The third child was Ruth, the boys' five-year-old sister, always the last to get a chance to speak. David was eight and Jonathan a year and a half younger.

"People just have different names for things," was their father's answer, leaving Ruth's question unanswered. "But they'll both be neat if he keeps going with that scythe." He pointed to the figure mowing part way down the hill.

David started to speak again but his father said, "Quiet, I love to see a man who can handle a scythe."

From the top of the rise where the wagon road curved toward Anson Stone's fields that lay beyond, Anson Stone stood quietly looking down the hill. Ruth had forgotten her unanswered question and had broken open a milkweed pod left over from the year before; she was blowing its feathery seeds to the wind. Jonathan was breaking a long stick into a dozen short ones. David was standing in thoughtful concern, exactly like his father except that he had one hand in his jackknife pocket and was gently caressing the two-bladed symbol that set him apart from "the children."

The higher-than-usual fence that separated the two graveyards on the same gentle hillside was the kind one might see around a private game reservation or park— or in front of a man's house to indicate to the world his bitterness toward life by his evident dislike for dogs and other people's children. The fence ran down the hill to the church and the sexton's house, ending at the corner of the sexton's vegetable garden. At the far end of the garden a gate came into the uncared-for graveyard, the burying ground. In order to enter it, one had to come by a rocky ford in the brook that lay beyond the sexton's house and the church.

Anson Stone had climbed his pasture fence from time to time to read the names and inscriptions on the small

stones and markers, some store-bought, some cast from
cement in rough homemade molds, some wooden crosses
of sawed lumber and some hewn out of locust wood by
hand. Under many, woodchucks had burrowed down
into the earth, causing them to fall and lie unnoticed in
the weeds and brambles.

On almost every store-bought stone there was a lamb
lying down or being carried in the bosom of a shepherd,
a dove with wings spread and an olive branch in its
beak, or an angel on a cloud. On one stone there were
two angels, one with short-cropped hair and knee-length
robes, and one with long flowing robes and hair trailing
in the wind.

But homemade or store-bought, the markers all car-
ried their message. The homemade ones had simple
carving: FEAR NOT, IN LOVING MEMORY, REST IN
PEACE. On the store-bought ones there were more elabo-
rate messages, but all were taken from the songs the
people had sung at their work, or from verses they had
cried "Amen" to in the Meetin' House: WHEN THE
ROLL IS CALLED UP YONDER, HE SHALL GATHER HIS
LAMBS TO HIS BOSOM, I KNOW THAT MY REDEEMER
LIVETH, HE GIVETH HIS BELOVED SLEEP, THE SLEEP
OF THE LABORER IS SWEET, I SEEK OUT MY SHEEP
WHERE THEY HAVE BEEN SCATTERED IN THE CLOUDY
AND DARK DAY.

At first, Anson Stone had read them because he was

curious. Later, he had re-read them many times for a feeling he couldn't exactly explain that made him feel good long after, as he walked to and from his fields. But for now he was curious about the stranger with the scythe that responded as though set to music, a black man Anson had never seen before.

A large pile of brush at the lower fringe of the lot indicated that the black man had already been over the lot and cut out the woody saplings that were too big for his scythe. So now the scythe in the demanding black hands moved in a gentle rhythmic arc and leveled everything before it.

The scythe, swinging from right to left, scarcely moved the man who held it. There was no reach at the beginning or sudden jerk or quick unbalanced foot movement as the scythe swung in its measured arc. A whispered swish was the only sound. There was no rattle of steel against stone or wood as the scythe slipped behind the grass and weeds that grew close to the grave markers. It seemed as though the point of the blade reached out like a finger to pull away whatever grew there.

A catbird fussed from the top of a mock-orange bush where the stranger had left a circle uncut so as not to frighten her from her nesting place. A song sparrow fluttered between a wooden cross and a sword-lily. Around the lily too an unmowed circle had been left.

David had grown tired standing like his father and, calling their collie after him, wandered out of sight around the bend of the wagon road to find the cows, for this was the purpose of the walk. Jonathan had been carrying on a contest to see how many of his short sticks he could throw over the pasture fence a few yards below the wagon road. Ruth had decided to imitate her brother, but with a stone that she would be sure to get over the fence. It sailed high above the fence and came down with a loud clack against a gravestone very close to the black man.

He looked up with such slow, deliberate calmness that Anson Stone felt that he must have been already aware that someone was near. If not that, then he accepted a stone being thrown at him as nothing unusual.

"I'm sorry," Anson Stone called. He left the road and moved down toward the fence. "My little girl was only aiming to outdo her brother, but she picked a flat stone that sailed much too far. She's sorry, too, and ashamed. I stopped to watch you handle the scythe. That's the best I've ever seen."

Ruth stood fixed by fear. Would the tall black stranger come at her Pa with his sharp scythe? Why did she ever try to copy the boys anyway? She wanted to run back along the wagon road and down through the orchard and be home. But her father had walked down the slope and was almost to the fence that separated the pasture and the graveyard. She would say one thing for her father, he was brave. He had walked right up to the fence and was leaning against a post. The black stranger could just reach over and cut off his whole head with the scythe. She reached for Jonathan's hand and tried to move back a couple of steps.

The black man rested his scythe against one of the wooden crosses, took a whetstone from his hip pocket, laid it on the arm of the cross, and stepped slowly up the hill toward the white man. As he came he wiped the sweat from his brow with the back of his hand. A red bandanna was tied close about his neck. His white-gray hair framed a face pronounced by lips rolled slightly outward and upward in a sensitive, questioning, subdued smile.

He stopped a few feet from the fence, looking past Ruth's father up to where she stood with Jonathan. His smile relaxed a little as he spoke. "Sometimes it's important for little girls to throw stones, especially if they have big brothers to keep up with."

How many times had her father said, "Don't try to keep up with the boys"? The stranger wasn't mad; in fact, he was on her side.

Jonathan was feeling better too. There had always been a question in his mind as to whether or not he qualified as a big brother. David had said he alone was old enough for that distinction. But David was out of sight getting the cows, and the man had called Jonathan a big brother, looking straight at him. Jonathan took a couple of steps to the edge of the slope so the stranger could really see how much taller he was than Ruth. And Ruth moved down toward her father and the black man with the slow smile.

The stranger's way with children was not lost to Anson Stone. But when the black man turned from the children to speak to the white man, the smile was gone. In his eyes was a gentleness and depth of light. To look into these eyes, floating in their dark sea and filled with understanding, was to feel the presence of a secret, and of a voice crying out in deafening silence—*discover me.*

Anson Stone reached a full arm's length through the fence. "I'm Anson Stone."

The black man took three quick steps forward and shook the white man's hand, saying as he did so, "I'm Moses Waters." And then he slowly moved back the same three steps.

"You're a stranger in these parts." Anson Stone noted that Ruth and Jonathan had come to the fence and were looking up into the eyes of the stranger.

"Yes sir, I've only been here a little while."

"You're doing a beautiful job at cleaning up—the—cemetery. Some of your people buried here?"

"No sir, but I thought I'd clean it up."

"I've even thought of it myself," Anson Stone replied. "Especially last summer when I came by and found a man who had come all the way from Washington, D.C., looking for his parents' graves. We checked every marker but couldn't find them. He said they had both died when he couldn't come back. He didn't say why, and he wasn't sure how long it had been."

"I'm going to teach the Cedar Corners school next winter," Moses Waters volunteered after a long pause. "I've just moved into the old Armentrout cottage about a mile past your farm. I come from downstate. But there they've started hauling the children who are left to the town school, and I'm not qualified to teach in the approved schools. My people are all moving away to the towns. . . ."

"You sure are good with the scythe. What'll you be doing 'til school time?"

"I was going to look for day-work after I finish this. And I want to whitewash the school and clean the cistern."

"Why don't you come to work for me? I've got work, and I like to keep my fence-rows clean. I can use you all summer."

"That would be good. It'll take me two more days to finish here. I can do the school and cistern between times."

The catbird was still fussing in the mock-orange.

Moses Waters turned his attention to Ruth and Jonathan. "I left a circle around her nest, but she's not very happy even so. That song sparrow is pretty mad too. But she's got the safest nest in the world—there in the top of the sword-lily. Do you know why it's called sword-lily?"

"No," Jonathan said, shaking his head.

"Its leaves are sword-shaped, and the edges are sharp. So sharp, they say, that a snake won't try to crawl up and rob the eggs from the bird's nest. The song sparrow knows that. That's why she built her nest there."

Anson Stone noticed that Ruth had pressed her face against the fence. The thought flashed through his mind that this teacher was pretty well qualified.

"It's Thursday. Would it be all right if I started Monday morning?" the black man asked.

"That'll be fine," the white man answered, raising his voice above the clatter of hooves as David brought the cows around the bend on the run, siccing the dog, Ranger, on them to make them go faster.

"I've told you not to run the cows," David's father called up to him. "They won't let down their milk. And Ranger's getting too old to run like that on a hot day."

A faint smile pulled back the corners of the black man's lips. The white man smiled too. "That is David, my oldest boy," Anson Stone said, pointing up the hill to the boy.

"Your children have good names," the black man said.

"Well, we better get along," Anson Stone said at last. "We'll see you Monday."

"I'll be there." The black man had untied the bandanna from around his neck when he came up fo the fence. While he talked to the white man he had wiped his face with it several times. Now he tied it back around his neck.

At the edge of the wagon road Jonathan whispered something to his father.

"That's a good idea," his father said half aloud. Then he called down to the black man, "You can save yourself a lot of steps by following the wagon road and coming down through my orchard instead of walking around the main road."

"I'm much obliged," Moses Waters called up the hill, lifting an arm with palm turned upward and nodding his head four times. As they passed out of sight of the black man, Anson Stone and his children listened to the measured metallic ring of the whetstone against the scythe.

"Who was that man and what were you saying to him?" David asked.

"Ruth almost got it. She threw a rock and it hit a gravestone right behind him," Jonathan spoke gleefully. "Lucky she didn't get her head cut off."

"That's not so, is it?" Ruth dropped back a step to walk beside her father.

"He's moved into the old Armentrout cabin, but it's falling down," Jonathan added. "He's going to teach the colored school at Cedar Corners."

"Who's paying him to mow the burying ground?" David asked.

"No one. But he's going to finish it tomorrow and the next day, and then come to work for us on Monday," their father answered.

Long after sunset Anson Stone saw the black man pass on the main road. He hadn't taken the shortcut along the wagon road after all. "Maybe he had to get something at the store," Anson said to himself, and he wondered if he would see the black man on Monday.

2

ANSON Stone didn't see Moses Waters pass during the next two days, but David, coming from bringing the cows, said he was still mowing.

But Ruth saw him. Sitting in church between her father and David that Sunday, she followed her regular routine. First she leafed through the hymnbook—that didn't have any pictures last Sunday or the Sunday before and wouldn't have any this, but she leafed anyway. Then she counted the windows on both sides of the church, and wished Mrs. Leech's baby would start crying as it always did. Then she twisted her head all the way around to count the four round pillars that held up the balcony.

When she finally got around to counting the balcony pillars, hoping Mr. Gordon was almost through his sermon, she saw the black man sitting alone in the balcony.

There was nobody in the two seats right behind, so she slipped her fingers up over the back of the seat and waved. She nodded her head and smiled. The artificial red cherries on her leghorn-straw hat rattled, and her father pushed his elbow hard against her side. But not before the black man had nodded and lifted his hand above the balcony rail and waved back with his fingers.

She wanted David to look, but when she punched him with her elbow, he only punched her back. She tried to look across in front of her father to motion to Jonathan but her Pa's elbow was there again, pushing her back in the seat all the way. Then the back of her knees ached because she couldn't dangle her legs over the edge.

But Mr. Gordon finally finished all the stuff she didn't understand. She was half a dozen steps ahead of the boys and her father by the time they got to the door. But the black man was already across the churchyard, heading toward the wooden walk-bridge. "He was in church," she said, pointing with her finger. "I thought Negroes had their own churches."

"They have; don't talk so loud," David whispered.

"But they don't have a preacher very often at the Cedar Corners Baptist Church," said their father, pushing her hat down on her head so it wouldn't fall off. "Besides, it's all right for him to come to our church. The same God's at both."

"He had on a suit," Jonathan said.

"What's so strange about that?" David asked disgustedly.

"I have never seen Negroes in anything but overalls."

"That's because you've not seen them on Sundays."

The boys wanted to walk home along the main road, but Anson Stone turned around the corner of the church toward the road that went up through the cemetery. He had built a stile over the fence. He liked to walk through his fields on Sunday. Then he didn't have to hurry. When they passed the burying ground he noted that the mowing was finished. All the fallen crosses and gravestones had been put back in place.

When Anson Stone came out the kitchen door and crossed the back porch after breakfast Monday morning, Moses Waters was leaning over the hen-yard gate. He was watching a wren as she fluttered in and out, luring a cat away from the nest she had built in a rusty pail which hung against the henhouse wall.

"Come on in and get some breakfast. I didn't know you were out here."

"I've been to breakfast."

"I've already milked. I milk before breakfast because there's a woman who comes in to work and that makes it better for her. Sure you don't want a cup of coffee?"

"No, thank you."

"We can turn the cows out and putter around the

barn until the dew dries off. Then we'll go into the fields. You see, I lost my wife last year, so I'm alone with the children. The woman who comes in is Mrs. Connors. She's the church sexton's wife and her children are all grown up, so it works out very well. She's a good worker but not very good with the children. Their questions ruffle her and she's short with them."

"Children have some pretty puzzling questions. They want to understand," the black man said slowly.

"Ruth asked me why you went to our church. I told her I thought we probably had the same God."

"I guess we do. I went by Saturday after work and asked Reverend Gordon if it would be all right."

Anson Stone had hooked his elbows over the barn-lot gate and was gazing past the barn where his fields rolled up the gentle slopes.

"I don't care much for Mr. Gordon, but there's nobody but me to take the children to church. Once when he paid a visit he said his wife wasn't feeling very well. I gave him a bottle of my three-year-old blackberry wine to take to her. The next Sunday he explained to the congregation how he poured it out on the ground—wouldn't have strong drink in his house. He didn't say who gave it to him but I thought he should have been man enough to say no when I offered it. Another time I gave him some Seventh Day Adventist tracts that I thought were pretty good. A few days later I found them blown into the fence corner of Ènoch Morris' garden. He'd thrown them away on the way home.

"Enoch Morris is a man you want to get to know. He's not like most people."

"I've already bought a few things at his store," Moses said. "The stovepipe was all rusted out and I had to replace it."

"But going back to the children," Anson said after a long pause. "Children live on love and dreams I guess. It was pitiful to see them all last winter. Hard. There's just no question that can be answered for a child about death. And I think they know more'n we think they know. During the months that she lingered I watched them change—little things like picking up their feet on the staircase, and not running through the house.

"It was like a storm that gathers slowly, almost without notice, and then destroys everything in its path.

"One night—it was about seed-catalogue time in January—I was watching a flame eat its way through a hollow apple log in the fireplace. She raised her chin from dozing and said, 'In a way I hate to think of spring coming and all the work. I feel tired all the time.'

"That wasn't like her at all.

"Always before, she could hardly wait for the ground to thaw and dry so she could get out and rake the leaves away from where the crocuses and daffodils started a cycle of bloom that she kept the door-yard bright with all summer. So I said, 'We'll see the doctor.'

"First it was a tonic and the doctor saying, 'We'll see.' But she kept going downhill.

"So the crocuses and daffodils showed among the dead leaves left over from winter. The day the first tree swallows came back, and the bleeding heart was in full bloom, we took her to the hospital for some tests. I took her the first lilacs before they were opened all the way.

"When we brought her home I put her bed by the window downstairs. All that summer long I used to come from the fields to turn her from one side to the other, when she had grown so weak. The nurse and Mrs. Connors did everything else. A brown thrasher nested in the rose trellis outside the window and sang from dawn 'til twilight. When the last fall flowers had been frosted and wilted and turned brown, she died.

"I've talked too long. The cows will think we're going to leave them in the barn all day."

Some animals get skittish when strangers come around, especially cattle and sheep. Moses Waters was a stranger, but he moved easily along the row of stanchions, rubbing the neck of each cow as he loosed the stanchion pin. Anson Stone had to prod them through the barn door. Here was a man, this stranger, feared by neither children nor animals. Anson Stone found himself pondering his feeling for the man.

The two men walked together behind the cows up through the orchard. All the way up not a word was spoken. Anson wanted to tell him some of the strange things that had happened during his dark summer of sorrow; but they could wait.

Finally the black man spoke. "Once Mr. Lincoln wrote to a little girl named Fanny McCullough, whose father he had known. He had died in the war. And I reckon Mr. Lincoln said about all there is to say about death: 'In this sad world of ours, sorrow comes to all; and, to the young, it comes with bitterest agony, because it takes them unawares. The older have learned to ever expect it.' "

Anson Stone had seen a mystery when he first looked into Moses Waters' eyes over the burying-ground fence. Now as he listened he wondered how long this man had walked the earth. By his gray hair he looked 55 or 60. But he was as straight as a pine tree in a crowded grove, strong enough to handle gravestones alone. Qualified to teach only in a left-over school, a shanty set on stilts in a part of the county sometimes called Cedar Corners but more often called "hard scrabble" because it was almost impossible to scratch a living from the land. "Patch of sour ground" it was also called, where a remnant of his people lived—less than a dozen families left over from squatter ex-slaves who had built their shanties on land white men didn't want after the war. Cedar trees were the biggest cash crop that grew in the rank acid soil, cut and peddled in the town for Christmas trees or sold as fence posts to the prosperous white farmers in the countryside. This man would teach a dozen or more children for a few years, until they were old enough to cut pulpwood for some white man or go to the mills in the town, his lessons forever silent in their hearts.

All this raced through Anson Stone's mind as he watched his new hired man close the gate behind the cows and turn from the orchard to the pasture, still speaking quietly as he moved. "Mr. Lincoln was right. Time is the great healer, and memory and loneliness the great purifiers. Memory is like an anvil with a hammer ringing on it, beating out the bends and warps of our minds. Loneliness is the furnace where the dross is smelted out and the stuff of memory softened so it can be shaped."

"I guess the dew has about dried off by now," Anson Stone said. "I noticed you brought your scythe and hung it on the hen-yard fence. I'd like you to trim the fence-rows in the fields where the hay has been gathered. The mowing machine can't get close enough, and if you don't do a little hand work each year the fence-row keeps creeping out, first the weeds, then brambles and sumac until there's a wide strip of wasted land. While we're this far we might as well walk on and I can show you where to mow; then we can go back and get your scythe. You'll want a jug of drinking water too. Mrs. Connors has dinner ready at twelve and supper at six.

She gets huffy if we're late for supper; she likes to get home. Have you got a watch?"

"No, but I can tell by the sun. But we didn't talk about arrangements, so my dinner is in a molasses pail down with my scythe."

"I'll give you two meals a day and the going wage, and breakfast too if you'd like." Anson Stone realized that this was the first time he had ever hired a man without a definite understanding. He felt a little uncomfortable mentioning wages to this man. He had never felt that way before.

Each man walked with his own thoughts. Along the way, Anson Stone pointed to a tall locust tree, stark without a single leaf, a dozen buzzards stretching their wings in the sun.

"We had a terrible hail storm last summer and lightning killed that tree," Anson said. "The leaves wilted and fell in a week. And the last leaf hadn't fallen before the buzzards came. They'd never been here before. Come to think of it, I never saw a buzzard in a tree that had leaves on it."

"They use air currents almost entirely for flight, that's why," Moses Waters said. "The bare trees don't disturb the air currents as a thick screen of leaves would. Watch as we get closer and they fly away; they'll just spread their wings and glide away. Not more than one or two will flap their wings. Buzzards never fight the wind;

they use it. Once they gain altitude, they use gravity to glide against the wind. They're ugly creatures to look at close up, with their bald heads, but they're beautiful in flight."

"There they go now," the white man said, pointing, "just as you said they would."

"They'll glide all the way across the valley," the black man said. "On the other side they'll start circling with the air current where it rises to pass over the hills; then when they get as high as they want, they'll set a straight flight pattern for where they want to go. Maybe right back to their dead tree when we have passed."

The white man watched closely. The buzzards did exactly as the black man had said they would. Anson Stone walked on with sudden admiration for something he had always looked upon with disgust.

When they came to the sharp corner of a pie-shaped field that bordered the cemetery, the white man stopped and pointed to an uneven mound of sod.

"David's pony is buried there," he said. "It happened last spring while his mother was still in the hospital. The horses cornered it between the cemetery fence and the bar-way and mauled it to death.

"For some mysterious reason David picked that one morning to come here to gather some lilacs, there along the cemetery fence, to take to school for his teacher. He found the earth-and-blood pulp of his pony, not one spot left to show the smooth grooming he had done with so much care each day.

"His grief struck him dumb. He came home colorless, and stammering so I could hardly understand. Later I found the lilacs for his teacher, lying in the mud at the edge of the red stain.

"He stammered terribly except when he said his prayers at night. When his mother came from the hospital he spoke to her also without a trace of stammer. The doctor said he'd get over it, said grief was always part fear, said he wasn't afraid of God or his mother and that was why he didn't stammer when he spoke to them. The doctor was right. The stammer left him in about six weeks.

"It came back for just a few days last fall when his mother died."

"I guess children have to stub their toes, fall out of trees they have climbed, and see these sad things, to be trained for living in the world," Moses Waters said as they paused at the bar-way that led into the hay field.

Anson wanted to ask Moses Waters if he had children, where they were, and a thousand other questions; but instead he said, "We'd like to keep children from these things, but you're right. They have to learn.

"I was telling you about the hail storm. This field was planted with wheat. It was almost ripe and ready to cut. Hail stones as big as guinea hen eggs flattened it. All we could do was mow it as best we could for hay.

"One day I was working here, and the children were playing along the fence; Ruth came running to me, crying her heart out and holding her eyes. I thought one of the boys had hit her across the face with a stick.

"She led me to a dead bobwhite mother that the hail had beaten to death. In a circle around her, their tails out and their heads under her spread wings, were sixteen dead baby birds.

"Then one night last winter, around the fire in the kitchen when everything was quiet and nobody had said anything to bring it about, she said, 'At least me and the boys didn't die with our mother like the baby bobwhites.'"

3

WHEN the two men got back to the hen-yard, where Moses Waters had left his scythe, Jonathan and Ruth were standing by the gate. Ranger, the black and white border collie, raced from the door-yard barking, the hair on his neck and shoulders standing upright. He took his place in front of the children. Jonathan rubbed his hand along the ruffled neck and back, and said, "Shut up, Ranger. It's all right."

"Ranger was sniffing at his dinner pail." Ruth said it to her father but looked up into the eyes of the black man. "David pried off the cover with his jackknife and looked in. I told him I was going to tell you, so he ran in the house when he saw you coming."

The black man smiled down at Ruth as he hooked the scythe over his arm and picked up the half-gallon molasses pail from the grass. Ranger wagged his tail and walked over for another sniff.

Anson Stone started to say, "Why don't you leave

your pail here, and come down for a hot dinner with us?" but he thought better and said, "I don't think David meant any harm."

When the black man was halfway through the orchard and out of hearing, Ruth turned to her father, "David said there wasn't nothing in the pail but three biscuits with fat meat on them. Ain't you going to get him for looking?"

"Suppose I did and he told Moses when he takes him a jug of water at the middle of the morning. You think that man, who thinks it's all right for little girls to throw stones at him, would think much of me?"

Ruth looked sheepish and found a convenient stick to fiddle with. She didn't know that her father had purposely not given Moses a jug to carry to the field himself.

Anson Stone went about his work for a while; then he decided he wanted to go to the store and talk to Enoch Morris. Enoch, he knew, had a quiet way of getting people to talk about themselves. Moses had been to his store. Perhaps Enoch had gotten the answers to some of the questions Anson had wanted to ask but hadn't.

It was a short walk and Ruth and Jonathan wanted to go, as they usually did, but Anson said, "No. I'm not going to buy anything. I just want to talk to Enoch a minute." David was still in the house.

When Anson Stone passed the back porch Mrs. Connors opened the kitchen door and called, "Is he gonna be eatin' here?"

Anson knew she referred to the black man. "Not dinner but supper," Anson answered. "But tomorrow he'll be having both dinner and supper." Anson would press the breakfast idea no further. He hoped the edge would be gone off Mrs. Connors' voice when the black man came into the house.

Enoch Morris was much older than Anson Stone, old enough to be his father. He was both store-keeper and farmer. His land lay across the road from Anson's, and his house was within shouting distance. His store was several hundred yards down the road from his house, where the main road ran toward the county seat ten miles away.

If this part of the county had a center it was the store; if it had a heart, it was Enoch Morris. He was a small, pink-cheeked man who wore thick eye-glasses and walked with a shuffle, as though he were not too sure of his next step. In his account book he had a long list of bills that were marked with X, indicating that he had given up hope of ever collecting them. But he believed that good could overcome evil in the world, that seeds of kindness, sown in stony and sour soil, would grow; and his belief could not be shaken. A stern, unrelenting sense of justice and a gentle love blended together to make this man. He might one night throw Mark Cowan out of the store for being drunk and disorderly, and the next day give him credit to buy winter shoes for his children, knowing that the chances of getting paid were slim indeed.

Anson Stone once referred to Enoch as the load-leveler, and when David had asked what it meant, his father had answered, "When something gets too heavy for ordinary men to carry, Enoch steps in and carries the extra weight. And I don't mean sacks of potatoes and grain, though he does that too; I mean troubles."

Four or five loafers sat on the store porch on nail kegs, spitting their tobacco juice over the rail of the porch into a stream that ran below. They were always there. In winter they moved inside and increased in number, and spat against the big pot-bellied stove that stood on a sheet of tin in the middle of the floor.

Enoch was inside alone, so he and Anson could talk without going into the little back room at the end of the store, where Enoch was usually motioned by whoever wanted to borrow money or tell him so-and-so was sick or in trouble.

"Yes, I sold him a scythe and a whetstone last week," was his reply when Anson asked if he'd seen much of Moses Waters. "And stovepipe and stuff to fix up old Armentrout's shanty several weeks ago."

"Has he been here that long?" Anson asked. "I had never seen the man until last Thursday."

"That was too soon," Enoch replied, smiling. "I went

up Sunday to ask him to work for me, and he said he'd already promised you. I told him that after me you were probably the next best man hereabouts to work for. No wonder you haven't seen him. He's been working from daylight to dark. And after dark. One night I heard what sounded like this loud tap-tap past my house and went out. He was passing, four 1 x 8 pine boards about 12 feet long on his shoulder. The ends flapping together were making the noise. He had carried them the whole three miles from Clark's sawmill. I took him the rest of the way in my pick-up truck but he was reluctant. Said he was used to carrying heavy loads.

"He'd be working for me today, except he told me that night all the things he had planned—fix his house, mow the burying ground. And I thought that would take half the summer, so I'd wait. The burying ground has been such an eye-sore for so long, and I was afraid he might come to work for me for pay, instead of working for the dead for nothing—if you can call it that.

"When I saw it was finished Sunday, I tried to catch him after church, but he got away too fast. Then I went up to his place after dinner to ask him.

"You should see what he's done to that shanty. Made it into a real cottage. Whitewashed it, painted the window and door frames green. Burned up all the trash that used to be piled sill-high around the house. Even the smell of sour-mash is gone from the place. Straightened up the porch with new posts. Built new steps. Even brought two little cedars from the woods and planted them each side the steps. Put a row of stones along each side the path to the steps. Mowed the whole lot as smooth as this floor. Said he'd measured his land, and it was just over two acres. Said the land is sour but he's already limed it to make it sweet. Even planted flowers to bloom next year. Except morning-glories—those he thinks he'll have climbing up his porch well before frost. Laid out a garden, square as a checker-board. Planted turnips. 'Got here too late for anything else,' he said. Cleaned all the dead wood and suckers from his five apple trees. Showed me where he'd cut into the base of one of his seven peach trees to take out a borer. Gathered pine pitch from the woods to rub on the cut. Said that would start the bark healing back over the cut. Then he walked out in the very middle of the lot and turned each way, pointing out the four corners of his land. Just like it might be Rube Flint's twelve hundred acres."

Enoch was excited, so Anson had to interrupt. "He's bought the place, then?"

"Yes, for almost nothing. When it was auctioned off in front of the courthouse to pay Armentrout's debts. Says he always dreamed of having his own place, and it took him until he was sixty-two years old to realize his dream. But you ought to see what he's done inside the house."

The morning was wearing away and Anson Stone wanted to get back to work, so he interrupted again. "Do you know if he has any family anywhere? How did he become so educated? He's been a teacher before, but he seems to know everything. And there's a lot of difference between book-learning and wisdom."

"Only folks he said anything about was a son. Sent him North and educated him as a doctor. Hoped he'd come back and heal among his own people, but he never did. Lives in one of the big cities up North. Didn't say which one.

"Know what he did with those pine boards he was carrying all the way from Clark's sawmill at nine o'clock at night? Built shelves for books. Cover one whole wall from floor to ceiling.

"Just as well that old Armentrout died in jail. He'd have dropped dead anyway if he'd ever come back and seen his house full of books.

"I'll tell you one thing, I think you've lost me for settin' this winter. I figure it's always better to talk to a man whose brighter'n one's own self if he's available," Enoch smiled.

"Settin' " for Enoch Morris meant stopping to visit with Anson Stone on winter evenings when he closed the store before bedtime. Everybody knew that Enoch's wife, Maggie, had a loose and acid tongue, which she used chiefly as a hammer to nail people to crosses.

Enoch lowered his voice slightly and continued, "One

of the Lawhorn tribe was in here Saturday night half drunk, laughing about how his uncle—old Armentrout was his uncle—must be turning over in his grave because a 'nigger's' moved onto his property. I told him Armentrout must have turned over right in the coffin before he was buried, knowing the Lawhorns had carried away his moonshine still before the corpse was cold."

Anson didn't care about continuing any discussion of the Lawhorns. "So the house is livable," he said. "I want to go up and see it."

"Got a new screen door," Enoch said. "Floor's clean enough to eat off of. Windowpanes where rags used to be stuffed. Curtains at every window. Says his next big job is to fence his land. He speaks with such feeling when he says 'my land,' I almost expected him to reach down and pick up two handfuls and let it sift through his fingers like it was gold dust."

"There's a lot of sour land in this country; it would be good to have a little of it sweetened," Anson mused.

"He wants to build a plank fence in front, with a picket gate. Wire around the rest. Said he always saw the place he dreamed of owning with a clean white-washed fence in front of it and roses climbing on it. I came right home and cut some slips from Maggie's roses to root in the hotbed. I felt sorta silly when I looked around at all the things my yard needs. I'll give them to him next spring."

Anson nodded to the tobacco chewers as he passed. He

would remember to tell Moses Waters that when he wanted more lumber from Clark's sawmill, he wouldn't have to carry it home on his back.

When he got home he filled a jug with cold water. He found David in front of the woodshed, trying to nail blocks together to make a birdhouse.

"Here, take this to Moses Waters. He's trimming the fence-rows in the first hay field."

"Can Jonathan and Ruth go with me? My arm'll get tired," David asked with a hurt softness, not looking at his father.

"No, they've got to help me move the sheep from the orchard to the hog-lot. The weeds are getting ahead of the hogs. I want the sheep to clip them down before they start going to seed."

David started off at a snail's pace, the jug pulling him over as though it were filled with stones. Anson Stone turned and walked the other way, calling for Jonathan and Ruth as he went.

He could have moved the sheep any time. But David must apologize himself for prying open the black man's dinner pail. He wouldn't have a chance to pay Ruth or Jonathan three marbles or his longest piece of string to do it for him.

Ruth stood above the path to make the sheep take the right turn. When her father came up to her, following behind the sheep with the bellwether leading them, she fell in with him and reached up for his hand.

"Mrs. Connors says she ain't never cooked for no ni—you know, what she called him," Ruth said, and turned her head to look up into her father's eyes. Her father's eyes showed no interest in this subject. He often changed unpleasant topics into pleasant ones, and he did so now.

"The next time I go to town I'm going to buy some more sheep-bells at Hawkins' Harness Shop. Don't you love the sound of the bells when all the sheep are walking in a straight line? We need about six more bells."

They walked on together, listening to the bells, following the sheep toward the open gate that led into the hog-lot.

David wasn't back until dinner was almost over. He had been gone two hours. He could have gone to the field and back in half an hour.

"Where—have—you been?" Ruth had reminded the boys several times that she'd be six in two months, and that "inside the house the women give the orders." And this was an order, not a question.

"Not anywhere," was all David had a chance to say.

"Eat your dinner; it's already cold. I don't wanta do two batches of dishes," Mrs. Connors said. Jonathan gave his father a faint smile and his father winked. Jonathan knew that David was safe.

When dinner was over Jonathan disappeared around the corner of the house and called David. Ruth followed.

"Weren't you afraid he'd get you for opening his dinner pail?" Jonathan asked.

"Didn't say nothin' about it."

"What'd he do?"

"Hung his scythe on the fence and came to meet me. Held the jug up and took a big drink. Then he said much obliged and carried the jug back along to where he left his scythe. Said water tastes best when it's brought fresh to the field the way I did. Said if you start the day with a full jug in the fence corner handy you take a drink every now and again and don't think about how good it is."

"He said that to you? What else?" Ruth looked around the corner to be sure her father wasn't anywhere near.

"He asked me when water tasted best for me, and I said I didn't know. He said, 'How about when you're sick with a fever, and you wake up in the dark and your forehead's wet with sweat and your throat's dry as a bone and you call out. Then you hear your'—he almost said mother but stopped—'father coming with the lamp in one hand and a cool glass of water in the other. Isn't that when water tastes better than any other time?'

"Then I said, 'You're right.' Then I told him I remembered a lot of times my mother had brought me a drink of water too."

"Didn't he sit down under one of the trees and drink

for half an hour like Mr. Connors and Ortho Drain do when they're helping Pa?"

"No, he just walked along the fence and showed me a bobwhite's nest with three eggs in it that hadn't hatched.

"I wanted to pick them up and bring them home, but he said they'd break in my pocket and smell. I knew he meant they'd stink like rotten chicken eggs. He said the bobwhite eggs probably slipped out from under the mother on a chilly night because she was covering anywhere from a dozen to eighteen eggs. Then he told me baby bobwhites can jump right out of the egg when they hatch and run after their mother. Said he didn't know any other bird that could do that."

"Pa wouldn't let us go," Jonathan said as he tore a plantain leaf into shreds and threw them to the wind.

"Why'd you stay so long?" Ruth asked.

"He kept talkin' and askin' questions while he mowed," David said. "He heard a dove far away in the woods and asked me if I knew why it took 24 days for bobwhite eggs to hatch and only 14 for dove eggs. I said no, so he said bobwhites lay a lot of eggs and raise only one family a summer, but doves only lay two eggs and raise three families in one summer. That's why they have to hatch faster."

"Let's take him some more water as soon as Pa goes somewhere," Ruth and Jonathan said at the same time.

"He can hear things a mile away. He said the dove was called a mourning dove because it had such a sad song. And some people call it the rain crow because it sings more when it's cloudy. He said there's always something to hear if you listen—even when it's quiet; then you can even hear the grass and the earth humming together if you hold your ear down to the ground.

"I watched him eat his dinner, too. He asked to borrow my jackknife to pry off the lid. Then he put my knife down on the lid. I knew he didn't have a cucumber to peel or nothin', so I thought maybe he forgot to give it back, but I was afraid to say anything. Then when he finished his dinner, he put the lid back on and took my knife and started walking along the fence. He cut an elderberry sapling and came back and sat under the locust tree. And guess what! Look!"

David reached deep into his pocket and held a clean white whistle up to his lips. He blew a shrill blast and put it back in his pocket, saying as he did, "And I ain't gonna trade it for nothin' you got, so don't ask."

Later Anson Stone rounded the corner of the house and stopped dead in his tracks. Before him, under the pear tree, lay three still figures, their heads flat against the earth.

"Are you sick?" he asked in alarm.

"No, we're listening to the earth singing," Ruth replied. "But Jonathan's kicking against it with his foot and that's all I hear. Make him quit."

Anson Stone waited what he considered a reasonable time for David to speak up and say he had apologized to Moses Waters. When nothing happened he walked away.

He hated inquisitive people who bluntly invaded others' lives. He tried to practice not doing it even with his own children. A little patience always got what he wanted to know from others anyway. And if his curiosity got the best of him, he always had Enoch Morris to rely on.

But with Enoch it was different, because it was important for Enoch to know things. In this part of the county there weren't more than a dozen or so who had telephones. So Enoch called the doctor when someone was sick; he closed the store and walked up the road or down it to tell somebody that a relative had died. He called the horse-doctor when somebody had a sick horse or cow. He called the bank to say that so-and-so was all right for a loan. He called the county treasurer to say that Mrs. East hadn't paid her taxes but that he'd be responsible for them. And what Enoch confided in Anson Stone remained between them only.

Anson walked along. Maybe he'd made too much of the dinner-pail lid, he thought. But David had seen enough field hands to know that no man ever bothered another man's dinner pail. What they reached from that dinner pail when they sat under a tree at eatin' time was their capital and their social symbol. If a man had a big piece of cherry pie or three sour pickles or an apple in addition to his biscuits, he laid them out on the open lid of the pail for all to see. One would hear statements like: "My ole lady bakes three pies a week." "I still got half a keg of sour pickle." "I'll have apples left over at pickin' time this year." If a man happened to have biscuits with the rich brown fringes of ham sticking from under the edges, he'd be sure to lift the top off the biscuit so everybody would get a whiff. But most of the biscuits had only a pale rind of sowbelly drooping from between them, and these were eaten quietly, without comment or show.

These distinguishing traditions existed only in the fields when numbers made it necessary for Anson to ask the hands to bring their own dinner, and where nature offered only one locust or persimmon tree along a fence line to provide shade for black and white workers alike. When there were few enough hands for a farmer to feed, the whites ate at the big round table in Anson's kitchen, the blacks at the wash-bench on the back porch.

Anson Stone knew that with Moses Waters it had meant absolutely nothing that a curious boy had peeped into his dinner pail. But David needed to know that, to some of the boastful harvest hands who would be around soon, such an act would be a personal insult.

Two hours before cow-time, Anson Stone looked up from following the cultivator through his waist-high corn and saw the three children, with old Ranger, pass around the hill toward the cow pasture and the hay fields, Ruth in the lead and swinging a jug at her side.

The cows, the children, and Moses Waters came home together at sundown. Anson Stone walked a few steps ahead as they left the barn after finishing the chores and started toward the house—the blast of three wooden whistles was deafening. On the back porch he picked up the plate, knife, fork, and tin cup put there by Mrs. Connors and carried them inside. He put them down between his place and Ruth's at the round table in the center of the kitchen. Mrs. Connors was still working at the stove.

When Jonathan had finished washing his hands a second time and finally got to his place at the table, Anson Stone asked the black man, who was standing with his head already bowed, if he would say the blessing. Mrs. Connors rattled the kitchen pump handle as she pumped cold water; its noise almost drowned out the soft voice of the black man:

"Lord, the psalmist said that you prepared a table for us, even in the presence of our enemies. How, then, can I thank you enough that I have the added blessing of sharing this table with friends? For all your blessings, more than the numberless tiny seeds from which this harvest of bread grew, we thank you. Amen."

During supper Mrs. Connors stayed busy washing

pans and rattling them in the tin sink. Her place at the table remained empty. Anson and Moses Waters talked about crops and weather. Anson told the black man how Enoch Morris had exclaimed, "You wouldn't recognize the Armentrout place, it's been fixed up so much." This gave Anson a chance to say, "Any time you need lumber or any big stuff let me know, and we can take my pick-up truck down to get it."

Long after Moses Waters had said, "I'll see you in the morning," and left the boys and Ranger who had followed as far as the hen-yard gate, Ruth and her father sat on the top porch step. Mrs. Connors went past them and grunted, "Good night." The pink glow of the sunset softened the fields and mixed the edges of the far hills with the sky above them.

"Mrs. Connors ate her supper in the pantry between times while she was washin' pans," said Ruth. "She said white folks don't eat with—"

"I know," her father interrupted.

"Do you think the earth sings, Pa?"

"I reckon it could. The stars dance, and the wind sings through the trees."

"In winter I've heard you say it howls."

"It's just the way we hear things at different times, I guess. Let's shut up the chickens before the dew gets on the grass."

4

IT was David's job to keep the wood-box filled, so when he heard his father making the fire in the kitchen stove, he hurried downstairs. So much had happened yesterday, he had forgotten to check the wood-box last night.

"I don't think Mrs. Connors will come to work," he said.

"She'll be here," his father replied. Anson Stone knew that Mrs. Connors' uppishness wasn't enough to offset her husband's laziness. Hatch Connors was the sexton at the church. He dusted once a week, and started fires in winter, but if there was a grave to dig, he managed to have "lumbago bad." He always got it at mowing time too.

Hatch was a nickname that had followed him ever since Enoch Morris got so tired of him loafing at the store that one day, right in front of a lot of people, he

41

said, "Why don't you go home and get to work, Ed? If you set here any longer you'll hatch out something for sure." Everybody laughed, and from that minute on he was never called anything but Hatch.

After his wife started to work for Anson, Hatch often found it convenient to show up just after milking time, when everybody was washing for supper. Anson would ask him to supper and he'd say, "I ain't feelin' very pert, but I'll have a bite." Then Jonathan and David would try to keep from snickering as he went through two helpings of everything, always reaching, never asking, sometimes barely missing the boys' plates with the elbow of his overall jacket.

Mrs. Connors came to work that morning as Anson had said she would, but Hatch never showed up at suppertime again.

When Moses had been working several weeks, Anson noticed that sometimes after supper he would walk to the store to buy sugar or coffee or nails, or maybe coaloil. One day Anson told him that when he needed something at the store to quit work a few minutes early and go over the stile and down through the cemetery, instead of walking all the way around the wagon road and then going back to the store.

After that, Moses arrived at suppertime several times with a bag of nails or a pound of sugar, so Anson knew he had followed this suggestion. But after a while Anson noticed that he changed back to his old way of going to the store after supper.

Anson got the answer from Enoch. "Hatch was boasting to his friends on the store porch," Enoch said, "about how he had allowed it a few times and then waited at the gate one day at sunset and said, 'You ain't supposed to trespass through here, nigger.'" He said a lot of people had stopped church because the nigger was comin'. So I went out and told Hatch the people that had stopped were probably the ones who hardly ever went except two Sundays before the church picnic and one Sunday before Children's Treat at Christmas."

But if Anson Stone and Enoch Morris worried about the world into which Moses Waters had moved, Moses never seemed to worry about it. For all Anson knew, it might even be a better world than the one Moses had known before. Anson always had a feeling that Moses thought he should walk alone.

Before the summer was over, Anson had hauled the lumber and wire for Moses to fence his land. The white plank fence and picket gate were built. The other three sides were enclosed with wire, protecting his trees and garden from varmints.

When he had found time to whitewash his schoolhouse, clean the cistern, and patch the stove with sheet metal where it was burned through, Moses asked Enoch if the School Board allowed any requisition for his school. Enoch lied to him and said, "Yes." So Enoch provided the slake lime and sheet metal that were needed, and a dozen window panes that had been broken during the summer.

Anson went the four miles to Cedar Corners to pick him up whenever he dared, but not every day. He honored the black man's independence and self-respect. On one trip he noticed that the stovepipe was badly rusted and very dangerous, since it ran the whole length of the room for added heat in the unceilinged room before it went through the wall. There was no chimney. When Moses took his advice and requisitioned it from Enoch, Anson Stone paid for it.

Once Anson said, "I want to give you two dollars a day. You're worth more than the regular dollar and a half wages."

"No, I just work like everybody else," Moses answered. And Anson knew not to bring it up again.

And Anson Stone knew there was no price that could be put on much that he owed this man.

Moses stood with Ruth in the orchard, watching a chipmunk gather apple-seeds, left by apples rotted from last year or the year before, and store them in a hole near the base of the tree. "Chipmunks raise their young in the early summer," he said. "Then they rest through the hottest weeks before they start storing up for the winter. When winter comes they just settle into their warm leaf-lined houses and have nothing to worry about.

"Field mice are different. They don't store away. That's why you see field mouse tracks in the snow, but never any chipmunk tracks. And you can always tell field mouse tracks from bird tracks because their tails leave little wavy lines in the snow right behind them."

Anson Stone's favorite spot for standing and dreaming on his farm was the top of the rise beyond the pasture where his fields spread before him to the woods and the far hills.

If the children had a spot which drew them more than any other, it was the smooth table rock halfway up the hill in the orchard. It stuck out of the ground about two feet, was easily twenty feet across and almost a perfect square. It drew Moses Waters too.

"I think some giants put it here long ago as a base for the statue of their god," Moses said to Jonathan the first time they had stood together and watched the lambs playing follow-the-leader up and over and around it. "No," he added, when the lambs had raced off through the trees and he sat on the edge, rubbing his hand against its smooth surface, noticing that Jonathan's eyes were demanding the rest of the story, "thousands or perhaps millions of years of wind and rain, sun and frost, have been making this rock just right for lambs to play on, and for boys to make a fortress of, and for a little girl to make a castle of, and for an old man to rest on." By the time he was finished, Jonathan's hand was moving gently back and forth over the even surface too, making sure the wind and rain, the sun and frost, had done a good job.

Moses knew it was time to change the subject. "The first morning I walked up here with your father, there were bluebirds flying in and out of that hollow apple tree. They're gone."

"Cat got them, I guess," Jonathan said after some hesitation.

"No. The young have grown up. Their parents taught them to fly from one apple tree to another until their wings were strong enough to fly over the fields. Then they flew across your father's fields to the big woods. That's where the parents are teaching the young birds to gather their own food.

"Bluebirds light in the grass to pick worms and bugs from the ground. So the parents knew it wouldn't be safe here.

"Besides, the parents wanted to go to the woods and hide for another reason. Carrying sticks to build their nest, going in and out of the hole in the tree, working from dawn 'til dark to feed their baby birds, they wore out their clothes. Their feathers got dull and frayed. So far over the fields, in the deep woods, they can keep their old feathers until they finish teaching their young. Then they change their feathers. That's called molting."

"All at once?" Jonathan was skeptical.

"No. You'd never see a whole bare spot on a bird the way you have on laying hens."

Jonathan couldn't remember having seen any, but he thought it better not to say so.

"Before long, about September," Moses continued, "they'll come back for a little while. We'll see them flying in and out of their old home, showing it to their children. Then they fly away to some elderberry grove and join a lot of their friends for the winter."

By now Jonathan was restless to make the fortress the black man had talked about. David was coming up the hill, and Moses knew it was time to go if he wasn't to get caught in the cross-fire of a siege.

The boys often had battles at the rock. Apples and sticks would fly over the wall. Someone, usually Jonathan, would cry, and there would be loud shouts and long silences. Then, just when Moses and Anson would begin to wonder, the warriors would come walking down the hill, too exhausted to run—the only condition under which boys walk in open land together side by side. A dozen steps before the gate David would put his hand on Jonathan's shoulder. By the time they reached the gate Jonathan wasn't going to tell his Pa that David had hit him over the head with a stick.

Ruth had her castle there too. The paths made by

the lambs through the grass to the flat stone were her roads, leading to the castle from so far away that no one knew how far. Along these roads all kinds of people came: princes, giants, knights, witches, good fairies, and lost children. The gates were kept closed against the bad and opened to the good. Under the castle there was a dark, mysterious dungeon where a beautiful princess was chained in a room that had no floor except the damp earth.

A row of trees near the rock was the dark forest. Ruth would come to the castle and spread out the treasures she had braved the monster-infested woods to bring back: three wrinkled pieces of bark to make curtains for a castle window, a fragment of caterpillar's nest for a queen's veil, a milkweed pod for a baby prince's cradle, and, for the crown jewels, seven tiny stones laid on a velvet cushion of four blue-jay feathers.

And at this favorite spot the black man paused once with David, listening to the sheep bells and watching the sheep peacefully grazing. Suddenly the sheep lifted their heads and raced toward a distant apple tree.

"Why do they do that?" David asked.

"They hear an apple drop, and even apples that are sour to us are sweet to animals. See how far away it dropped—four trees along the row. We wouldn't have heard it if we'd been just at the next tree. They had their heads down close to the ground. They're blessed with keen hearing.

"You know in the Bible where you read about all the shepherds bringing their sheep to the same watering hole?"

David didn't know, but he almost believed he did, so he said, "Yes."

"There were no fences, so the flocks would all be mixed up together, milling around. But this didn't bother the shepherds. They would sit under a tree together and talk. Then when one shepherd decided he'd visited long enough, he would walk up on the hillside and start calling, 'Rachel, Rachel,' which in his language meant 'little ewe.' Each flock knew its own shepherd's voice, and they would leave all the rest of the sheep and go up the hill to their shepherd. That's why the Bible says, 'The sheep know the voice of the shepherd, the stranger they will not follow.' They also know the footstep of their own shepherd. That's why it says, 'The thief enters not by the gate of the sheep-fold, but climbs the wall and enters by another way.' The Almighty wanted people to have a keen sense of hearing, and hear His voice like the sheep hear the voice of the shepherd and follow him."

That night before they fell asleep David told Jonathan the story of the lost sheep, and of David the shepherd boy. From far away, in the upper corner of the orchard, a sheep rubbing against a tree to get rid of a tick set a single bell tinkling, smoothing out the night with music for the boys to sleep and dream by.

In midsummer Jonathan followed into the corn-field when Moses went to look for a stray calf that had crawled through the pasture fence. The corn was as tall as the man, shutting out the sun in the shade below, where Jonathan ran two steps and walked one to keep up. While Moses scanned the rows for the calf, Jonathan glanced about to see if there were giants or Indians lurking among the stalks. Moses picked a woolly worm off the corn and showed Jonathan how to measure the narrow or wide brown stripe that told whether or not the winter would be short or long.

Then Jonathan stepped on a broken bottle and cut his bare foot to the bone. Moses made a tourniquet of the red bandanna which he always wore at work, bound the cut with the handkerchief from his pocket, cradled Jonathan in his arms. The tears that had made two dirt-streaked rivulets down Jonathan's face were dry by the time Moses had answered three questions.

"Will I have to get it sewed up?"

"Yes, but the doctor will put something on it so it won't hurt."

"Will he let me walk on my heel?"

"Yes. He'll put a bandage on it that won't come loose, and you'll walk right out of his office."

"Can you carry me all the way home or will you have to put me down and go for Pa?"

"Big boys don't feel so heavy when they're hurt. We'll make it all the way."

Jonathan reached out awkwardly to touch the passing blades of corn. The silken green rubbed against his cheek. After a while he spoke. "I love it when the corn-blades rub against my face; they're cool and soft."

At the edge of the field the black man rested his burden on one knee; he brushed his calloused hand over the boy's wet brow and pushed back the sweat-matted hair from Jonathan's eyes.

Through the pie-shaped field, along the cemetery fence and the wagon road, down through the orchard, Moses Waters carried the child home. Without calling out alarm from halfway up the hill, keeping the identi-cal pace at which he came from work, he arrived at the door-yard. Jonathan greeted his father with a faint smile.

On the way back from the doctor, they stopped at Enoch's store to get Jonathan some stick candy. "What-ever Moses does he does for the sake of the thing he is doing, not for himself," Anson Stone said to Enoch.

All summer long David, Jonathan, and Ruth listened to Moses Waters' stories, followed at his heels, and watched his hands as they unraveled the mysteries of where the honey was stored for the hummingbird in a trumpet flower, where the life-cell lay in a bud or acorn, and how old the tree was that he was splitting into fire-wood.

These same black hands brought dignity and grace-fulness to whatever he did. If he dug a post-hole it looked as though it had been bored with an auger, and the earth he removed piled up to make a toy pyramid. If he pruned a grape-vine each new stem he wished to mature was left with three buds. If he built a fence it was straight enough for a bullet to follow. If he chopped a log the cut was as smooth as a saw-cut, and even the chips looked as though they had been measured to diminish at a given width and angle. If he set bean poles in the garden they all stood at the same height and in a perfect line. If he dug a ditch its sides and bottom made right angles as if they had been marked out by a carpenter's square. When he cleaned a field of hay there were no gleanings left for horse or cow or sheep to gather.

Whatever tool he used was always wiped clean and put back in its proper place. He had retained the ancient closeness of work and worship that, as Anson and Enoch had so often lamented, seemed otherwise to have disappeared from the earth.

Anson Stone noticed a change in the boys as the summer deepened. Before, he had always had to pick up the saw and hammer used to make a boat or birdhouse, or the garden hoe left in the middle of the row when somebody decided "I'll finish later" but never did. Before the summer was gone it came to him that he hadn't picked up any tools for quite a while.

One evening after work the two men stood by the door-yard gate. The summer was ending. The sky that had seemed close enough in June for the swallows to brush their wings against, or for a boy lying in the grass on a hill-top to punch a hole through with a stick, now seemed far away.

Anson was thinking of the past lonely winter. How helpless he had felt then, trying to fill up the cold emptiness that crept through the house. How different it had been since he had paused to watch a stranger mowing among the dead.

Soon the school year would begin. He knew that Moses' teaching pay would be forty-five dollars a month for an eight-month school year.

"Why don't you come by after school and help me with the chores?" he said to Moses. "The children need you too."

"I'll come," the black man said as he turned to leave.

Ranger squeezed through the gate and walked before him. Every evening he trotted along with his friend through the barn-lot and up the road to the end of Anson's land. And in the morning he would go to that same spot and be waiting when Moses came to work.

Some dogs are owned by people; but not collies, and more especially border collies. They own the people whom they love. During the summer Ranger had come to own Moses Waters, as Moses Waters had come to own them all.

5

For David and Jonathan school was old stuff and Anson had a hard time getting them to find their lunch boxes and book satchels, which neither had seen since June. But Ruth was bursting with excitement. It was her first day of school. She was downstairs in her new dress before Anson had finished building the fire.

When Mrs. Connors came and Ruth walked in front of her and said, "Look at my new dress," all Mrs. Connors said was, "Did you wash your neck before you put it on?" This didn't bother Ruth because Mrs. Connors always had her hackles up. The only thing that kept the day from being perfect was that she had to wear shoes.

"Why do I have to wear shoes before frost? I learn with my head, don't I?" she had asked her Pa at supper the night before.

Moses smiled when Anson didn't answer but Jonathan said, "The kids will tromp on your toes in line, that's why."

And David said, "You can't kick back if you ain't got shoes."

She asked Mrs. Connors to tie her shoes, but she saved her hair-ribbon for Pa to tie when he came from the barn.

Just before time to go to school, Ruth went to the barn to show Moses her new lunch-box with a "Mary Had a Little Lamb" picture painted on both sides, and her new book satchel—blue canvas trimmed in leather, with a special compartment for pencils.

"You're as pretty as a flower," Moses said. He patted her lightly on the head. "Now you can bring home some stories to tell me."

Anson Stone walked with the children to Enoch's store. There they waited for the school bus. They lived more than a mile and half from the school and were entitled to ride. Anson had wanted to go all the way for Ruth's first day of school, but Ruth had said, "I might cry when you leave me, and all the kids would laugh." David had warned her beforehand: "Don't let Pa come. Only mothers bring their kids the first day."

At Enoch's store Anson bought three jumbo-lined writing tablets and three No. 2 lead pencils with cap erasers. David sharpened his pencil with his jackknife over the store porch railing, and when he got a good writing point his pencil was only about half as long as when he started.

When the bus stopped across the bridge, Ranger

trotted in front of the running children and stood by the bus door until it closed behind them. For the two years since David had started school, Ranger had come in the morning, and in the afternoon he would be waiting. He would leave Anson at home or in the fields, and judged exactly the time needed to get there and be waiting.

"You ought to get a new young dog to grow up with Ranger before he dies; he's getting pretty stiff with age," Enoch said as the two men stood watching the dog take a longing look after the bus and make his way back toward them.

"I'll get one next spring," Anson said. "Was planning to do it this summer but it slipped my mind. The summer went so fast."

Enoch watched Anson and the dog disappear around the bend of the road. He hoped no one would hurt the children at school. The day before, Mark Cowan had been boasting to his tobacco-chewing friends on the store porch about how he had a kid starting to school and was going to send a note to the teacher and tell her "not to let his kid set near any of them Stone kids 'cause they're livin' around a nigger all the time and probably got cooties."

When Enoch had stood about all he could, he had said, "And just who are you going to get to do the writing for you, Mark?" Enoch knew that when Mark got his old father admitted to the poor-house, both he and his wife had signed with an X. Enoch hoped Cowan's remarks would never get to Anson.

Enoch heard a clear "kee-ee-er, kee-ee-er" high in the sky above the hills. His glasses were for short sight so he couldn't see, but he knew what it was—a red-tailed hawk calling her young in for the kill.

When the bus came from school, Enoch made it a point to be out on the store porch. "I think a little missie"—he called all girls "little missie" and all boys "little man"—"deserves a treat after her first day at school," and he held out two red-striped sticks of candy; then one each to the boys, saying as he did, "So you won't push her in the brook before you get home."

The first days of school were exciting. Ruth spread out her new reader on the kitchen table and looked at the pictures. The book was called *Adventure Circles*.

Looking at the pictures, Anson noted that the adventure circles led from the school to a firehouse and back to school, from a house to a grocery store and home again. He also noted that the same person had all the adventures. Her name was Jane. When Ruth tired of Jane's adventures after a while, Anson was not surprised.

One night after supper Ruth announced that she knew all Jane's adventures. But when Anson covered the picture with his hand, any one of several adventures, not on that page, might be "read."

The next day he asked Moses if he would stay and

study with the children an hour after supper each night for the regular wages. Moses said, "Not for wages." Anson said, "Wages or wages and a half." So they reached an agreement.

Moses began to study with Ruth about the same time his own school started. He had only fourteen scholars, but thought he might get a few bigger boys when crops were in and pulpwood cutting slowed down. Some of his young ones walked several miles, and there was no bus for the Cedar Corners school, so he thought he would lose a few when bad weather set in.

Anson Stone found excuses to be up Cedar Corners way at school letting-out time whenever he could. Moses was always glad for the ride and never asked Anson why he bought only three fence posts at a time. Enoch Morris issued pencils and writing tablets on the School Board's requisition. David almost got Enoch caught one night when he told his Pa he needed a penny the next morning to buy a pencil.

"I thought the School Board supplied pencils and paper," Moses said.

"But not stick candy," Anson answered, and changed the subject.

Moses always carried some books that had brown wrapping-paper covers on them and not many pictures inside. Ruth asked her father if all of Moses' stories came from "those wore-out books."

Anson watched a great change come over the approach to learning at the kitchen table soon after Moses started reading with Ruth. Ruth could hardly wait to get Mrs. Connors out so they could start. She even started helping wipe the dishes to hurry her. Anson and the boys liked this. The kitchen always seemed to be a little warmer with Mrs. Connors gone.

Jonathan and David began to get their books out without being told. Sometimes there was a little pushing to see who would sit at Moses' other side. They began to bring home books which were supposed to be used only at school. They searched the black man's "wore-out books" to find the stories he had told. They did find some good stories, but his stories were all from other books.

Anson Stone marveled at the skill of the teacher, kindling fires that made eyes glow and hearts hungry. He handled young minds and hearts with the same skill he used to make a scythe sing, or a plant grow in sour ground. No movement of a child at play, no look of joy or hurt, was lost to him.

"David is really a quiet child," he said to Anson once, when David's voice was filling up the whole orchard as he bossed Jonathan and Ruth around. "He will be a silent man; he has still courage. It demands so much of him that he rebels against it. But it stays inside him, and everything will happen to him inside. When he plays alone he is his real self. He thinks of his mother a lot . . . .

"Jonathan lives in a cautious world that his sensitive heart has made. He measures and sizes up things as the other children do, with the question: 'What can I do with this?' But Jonathan goes further and asks a second question: 'What can this do to me?'. . . .

"It seems to me that whoever picked Ruth's name when she was born knew how she would grow up. Her name means beautiful companion. She shakes off the bad and finds some good in everybody."

And while Moses was still talking, Ruth ran to her father ahead of Jonathan who was crying, saying as she ran, "David didn't mean to push him that hard."

A simple story of Achilles ploughing behind his oxen in a land named Greece would bring the smell of brown earth in April up from the page when Moses touched it. He could move Greece across the sea in an instant, and Jonathan would be in a world he knew, up through the orchard to the fields, following Achilles behind the plough, with fat robins gathering worms.

"Why does the story tell about robins following Achilles' plough? How do you know there were robins that long ago?"

"God made birds to follow after ploughs and gather

worms. The birds might not have been robins, but I don't think God would cheat Achilles, do you?"

"Was his plough like Pa's?"

And what had started as a simple story far away came to the kitchen table and was transformed into a whole chapter in the history of mankind.

"No, in the beginning the plough was just a strong forked stick. Achilles' plough probably had better handles than earlier ones, but it still had a wooden point and didn't do much more than just scratch the earth.

"Men had iron then, but they used it to make swords. Ask your teacher if she thinks the world would be much different today if ancient men had used iron to make ploughs instead of swords and spears.

"The first iron plough-point was invented by a poor English serf—that's something like a cross between a hired hand and a slave—whose master kept beating him for not ploughing deep enough.

"Only about a hundred years ago a man named John Deere invented a plough like the one your Pa uses. He was a blacksmith in Vermont, where the hills are stony and hard to plough. When word came back that there was a place called Illinois where you could plough all day and not hit a stone, John Deere decided that was the place for him. He was sick and tired of fixing ploughs all the time in his blacksmith shop.

"When he saw the smooth prairie soil, he decided it

deserved something better than just scratching. So he invented a plough that would plough a foot deep and turn up rich black furrows to dry in the sun."

And when Moses had finished the story, a little bit of reverence for earth and respect for the tasks of living burned in the eyes of the children. And come spring, Anson Stone would follow his plough, turning long straight furrows in his fields, and not grow as tired as he used to.

A small cloud the size of a man's hand, rising above the horizon in the brightest part of the sky, may foretell a storm.

One afternoon Moses Waters came from his Cedar Corners school early. Someone had broken the handle off the cistern pump. Would Anson drive him to town to buy one?

"I need to go anyway," Anson said. "Ruth needs a new coat. We'll go by the school and pick her up."

In front of the school they waited until the bell rang and the children marched through the door, then broke into a stampede in every direction. Anson walked toward the bus and called Ruth.

"I have to go to town. If you come we can get your new coat."

David and Jonathan had arrived by now. "Can we go too?" David asked, starting toward the truck.

"Not this time. Moses is with me, so you'll have to start the work. We'll be a while."

There was no excitement in Ruth's eyes. She was looking over her shoulder to see how many people were still on the school ground. "I wanta go with the boys," she managed in a sheepish half-whisper.

"Don't you feel well?" Anson asked as he took her by the hand and led her out of the path of children pushing and scrambling to their favorite seats in the bus. "I never knew a time when you didn't want to go to town. We'll buy your coat, and Mr. Weinberg will give you an all-day-sucker. He always does."

"Can we wait 'til all the kids leave? If they see, they'll yell bad names at me tomorrow." And she began to sob.

"Nobody would do that! Has anybody ever done that to you?" But now they were almost to the truck and she didn't answer.

Moses noticed her tears and said, "Did somebody push you?"

"Yes." She climbed up under the steering-wheel and sat between the two men.

"What color new coat do you want to buy?" Moses asked.

"I'm not sure."

"I think you should have a red one and a muff to match. Then you can be Little Red Riding Hood," the black man said.

Ruth and Moses talked about Little Red Riding Hood and the wolf. Moses thought there were lots of Little Red Riding Hoods, but not many wolves. Ruth wasn't sure.

Except for wondering out loud what kind of person would break a handle off a cistern pump and throw it away, Anson Stone was quiet all the way to town.

Mr. Weinberg didn't have a red coat with a matching muff. But he had one with a black velvet collar and wrist-bands, with matching red mittens that hung around your neck on a long piece of black braid. "Long enough to put your mittens on and in your pockets at the same time," he said. So they bought that one.

Mr. Weinberg gave Ruth a big hug when he finished buttoning up her new coat. And he gave her two all-day-suckers from his inside coat pocket that he had put there when he saw them coming in the store. "One for each hand," he said.

He asked about Enoch Morris. "We've been friends for years," he told Moses. He asked Moses about his school, and Anson said, "Which one? He has two schools. One's in my kitchen." Moses told Mr. Weinberg his school was fine. He didn't mention that somebody had broken the handle off the cistern pump and thrown it away.

Before they got to the hardware store, Anson said, "The County Board probably won't have requisition rights in here."

"I thought not," Moses answered. "I've got the money."

On the way home, Ruth and Moses talked about her new coat and how nice Mr. Weinberg was. Anson didn't say much. He wanted to ask Ruth some questions, but they were questions he hated to ask. She had forgotten all about the thing that was bothering her father so much. He would get her alone and ask her before supper. If he waited until after Moses had gone home, she might go to bed upset.

Anson thought he would make an excuse to go back to the barn while everybody else was washing for supper and call Ruth after him. But when he came from the barn he changed his mind. Ruth was walking around the kitchen, her new coat still on, her hands, with the mittens on, stuffed deep in her pockets.

"This has been one of my best days," she said.

After supper when books were spread out on the table, and everybody was busy, Anson Stone discovered he needed something from the store. Before an inquisitive child could ask what it was, he was out the door. He needed to talk to Enoch.

"I think my children are being mistreated at school," he said to Enoch when they had passed the grizzled loafers perched on nail kegs around the pot-bellied stove and Enoch had closed the door to the back room. Then he told Enoch why Ruth hadn't wanted to go to town when she saw Moses in the truck.

The color drained out of Enoch's face. It took on a cold, ashen color that Anson had seen only once before —when Enoch took a buggy whip to Doc Robinson. Doc was county coroner, but had no license to practice medicine; he held the county job illegally. Loaded with either liquor or morphine, he had run his horse to a white lather. When the horse stopped in front of the store and refused to move, old Doc had gotten out and started beating it over the head with the butt end of the buggy whip. Enoch took the whip from him and horsewhipped him. Then Enoch threw the whip over the bank into the brook.

"You'll have to go to the school and speak to the teachers," Enoch said after a long time.

"I hate to meddle into school things. It could spoil a child. Teachers can get soured too; they don't like meddling parents. And the children are doing so well in their books this year."

Enoch was always ready with a sermon. So now he launched into one: "This world is full of hunger. There's soul-hunger, greed-hunger, and hate-hunger. If a man has soul-hunger, he feeds his soul; if he has greed-hunger, he feeds only his head; if he has hate-hunger, he eats up his own soul, and carries a bitter taste in his mouth for the rest of his life. This county's got an overdose of hate-hunger."

"I'll think about going to the school," Anson said after they had walked through the store and were standing on the porch. The November stars looked far away.

"There's a few people in the world who can feed both their souls and heads at the same time. They're the few that end up with educated hearts." Enoch wanted to continue, but Anson interrupted. "Good night, Enoch," he said. "I've got to go; Moses will be wantin' to get home."

"I wish all teachers were like him," Enoch called after Anson. "He's one man who's got an educated heart."

Anson watched for a sign. For two days he managed to get each of the children alone after school and ask, "How was school today?" The answer from all three added up to "Good," with details of what they'd learned or who in the class was dumb.

Anson had about decided that he'd probably imagined too much. After all, they had to learn sometime to take a few knocks. He wouldn't meddle.

But on the third day Ruth brought a note from her teacher. The teacher would like to speak to him.

Ruth said, "Why don't you get there after all the kids are gone? I don't have to stay, do I?"

"No, she didn't say you had to be there. She wouldn't want you to hear her say you're ahead of the class. That would give you a swelled head, or bust a button off your coat collar from sticking out your neck."

The conference at the school began with an opening which Anson had come to expect as standard.

"I understand what a difficult task it is to bring up children without a mother, Mr. Stone."

"Our situation has improved this year. A wonderful neighbor and friend has moved just up the road from us. The children enjoy their new friend. He has the knack of making them feel grown without becoming smart alecks. What seems to be Ruth's problem?"

"It's a problem of adjustment in her age group. From almost the first day of school I noticed that she didn't enter into play with the other children of her age group. I thought it was something that would pass. But I notice that she still plays alone at recess or follows after one of her brothers. And now she is becoming something of a problem in class. All the other children are happily adjusted socially and do their work together, except Ruth. The problem has increased recently because she is not reading with the class."

"Behind or in front?" Anson Stone asked, smothering the sparks that tried to jump off the end of his tongue.

"Ahead," the teacher said, "but she has developed the disturbing habit of partial visual application. She reads without studying the picture as she reads. That lets her move ahead of the group. She has also taken home her in-class reading book which is only for coordinated class use. And she has told the other children most of the stories in it, taking away their interest and anticipation. These are all indications of frustrations expressed by non-conformity that should be closely watched."

Anson Stone had a strong stomach, but right now he felt a little squeamish. "She likes to read a lot at home. But I thought that was good. I'll have to keep her busy at other things, I guess."

"While you're here, would you like to speak with Jonathan's and David's teachers?"

"I suppose I might as well."

Jonathan's and David's teachers were waiting.

Jonathan's teacher was equally disturbed. "Jonathan is a very likeable child, Mr. Stone, but he makes it difficult for the teacher to teach the other people in the class. He wastes valuable time by continually holding up his hand to supply little aside facts. Just today, for example, he upset the social studies class by pointing out that the picture of Washington crossing the Delaware was incorrect. It showed a soldier standing at the front of the boat holding an American flag. Jonathan insisted that when Washington crossed the Delaware there was no American flag."

"Well, was he right or wrong?" Anson asked, in a voice that was almost a whisper.

"Yes, of course, he was right, but that's not the problem. That kind of thing tends to alienate him from the rest of the class. Somebody blurts out 'smarty.' Then others snicker and the snickers are carried through the rest of the day. It is not good for the other members of the class to feel that one member knows something they don't. Someone might feel left out, and develop an inferior feeling or a sense of hopelessness toward learning.

"It is affecting his relationship on the playground too. I had to go out once and stop the boys from jeering at him for playing with the girls."

David's teacher was only slightly disturbed. "I allow the children to do their arithmetic on scratch paper and turn in answers only. This increases their ability to recall. David does not follow instructions. David insists that he should put down each individual step of the problem. He also introduces a great many colloquialisms and fabrications into the stories he reads. For example, there is a little story in his reader about Achilles, based on the *Iliad*. He used the whole class story period talking about ploughs! So none of the other children got a chance to tell what they had *read*. Outside of class he seems to be well adjusted socially."

"It could be worse," Anson said, leaving long gaps between his words. "But not for me. If David didn't do enough I'd know how to handle it. This way I don't really know what to do. But thank you anyway. I'll try."

On the way home Anson Stone analyzed his problems. He had only two: to find out why Ruth didn't play with her group, and why Jonathan played with the girls. Moses Waters already had solved the other problems.

At home all the work was finished. The wood-box was full, lunch-boxes washed and drying on the sink, book satchels brought in from the porch.

Moses almost never went into the kitchen except with Anson Stone while Mrs. Connors was there. He was waiting on the porch.

"That young heifer had her calf," he said, "I didn't tell the children because she's pretty skittish."

"What'd she say?" Ruth asked before her father was through the door.

"Just what I told you she'd say—you're ahead of the class."

"Did you see my teacher?" David and Jonathan asked together.

"Yes, I did," Anson replied smiling. "I've got to raise Moses' studying wages. You're all ahead."

When supper and studying were over and Moses had said goodnight, Anson Stone pushed his chair back from the fire and lifted Ruth up to his lap.

"Your teacher says you read ahead of the children in your class but you don't play with them on the school-ground."

"Most of 'em aren't very nice."

"What do they do?"

"Push me off the bench at lunchtime and say, 'You can't eat with us 'cause you eat with that man.' "

"When?"

"The first day of school and since."

"Anything else?"

"They push me out of line and say things. They say, 'Don't stand too close or we'll catch cooties.' What are cooties? And they hurt me once. They made me fall and cut my lip."

Anson Stone squeezed her arm a little tighter. Her lower lip seemed too heavy to hold up, so he put a finger lightly against it. If he had not occupied his hands for this, he would have grabbed the fire irons from where they stood against the chimney and broken them like kindling wood over his knee.

"Do they still do it?"

"Not much. When I wore my new coat they said, 'Red ain't white people's favorite color, but you ain't got no Ma to help you.' And then I ran away."

David and Jonathan sat fixed at the table. David pretended that he was reading.

"Why do you play with the girls in your grade instead of the boys?" Anson Stone asked Jonathan.

"They don't call me that name."

"The teacher said she stopped them from jeering at you."

"That's when a pigeon hawk dive-bombed a starling where it was eating lunch crumbs and killed it. They were trying to put the dead bird in my pocket. Said, 'Here, you like blackbirds, you can have it.' I took it away from them and two of the girls went with me to bury it. They kept yelling that name 'til the teacher stopped them."

"What else?" Anson asked.

"They rub my coat collar in line and say, 'Whoever saw a coat collar made outa kinky fuzz. See, kinky just like a woolly head,' and then I started a fight."

Anson had bought him a cossack-style coat with an imitation Persian lamb collar. It was one of the nicest coats Mr. Weinberg had, and had cost more than Anson Stone planned to pay. But after Jonathan had tried it on the third time, Isaac Weinberg had said, "Take it—with twenty per cent off."

Now it was David's turn.

"Why don't they bother you?" his father asked.

"They did at first."

"Why'd they stop?"

"There was this squirrel hole in one of the maple trees, and they said if I had courage enough to climb it and put my hand in the squirrel hole they'd stop. So I did it. Squirrel bit clear through my finger but I didn't cry."

"Why didn't you tell anybody and get it fixed?"

"I told Moses and he put some turpentine on it. I didn't tell him why I did it. Just that I did it to show that I had courage. He said he didn't think it was as much courage as foolish. Then I asked him what courage was, and he said it was different things. Said sometimes courage was just being a child. I asked him what he meant, but then you came in the barn and he put the turpentine bottle back on the shelf and stopped talking."

Sap escaping from a stick of green wood burning in the fireplace, usually music for a man to doze and dream by and conjure up pleasant visions, now took on the hissing sound of a wounded serpent, its fiery tongue striking wildly and blindly in its death throes. The cold loneliness that Anson Stone had felt once before, when his world collapsed, had crept back into the kitchen. David got up to get a drink of water.

"Light the lantern," his father said at last.

He's going after the Cowans, the Lawhorns, and the Kecks, and they'll shoot him down in the road like they did Ron Hartbarger, Jonathan was thinking to himself. Jonathan had been at Enoch's store with his Pa when the sheriff brought Ron's body by in the back of his pick-up truck. Remembering, Jonathan felt his lips quiver and his eyes fill with tears. He imagined his Pa lying face up in the back of the sheriff's truck.

"You can't go," he burst out at last, falling at his father's knees and wrapping his arms around them.

"We're all going," his father said. "Moses didn't tell you, but there's a tiny new spotted calf in the barn."

On the way back from the barn, David, who was leading with the lantern, stopped.

"Listen," he said. "Hear that hoot owl?"

From far beyond the fields the weird oot-too-hoo, hoo-hoo sent chills up and down their spines.

"Moses says the owl does that after he's finished feasting on a rabbit or a bobwhite. Says he does it to scare the rabbits and bobwhites to cover. Then other owls will go hungry; and he'll come back and catch another one tomorrow night. Moses says he's one of the greediest birds."

Back in the house Anson Stone put the fire screen in the front of the fireplace. The green wood had given up trying to burn, and lay smoldering in the ashes.

"We're up too late," Anson said. "Time to bed down like a spotted calf full of warm milk."

Fragments of whispers on the stairway came down to the man standing alone in the hall. *Why didn't you say they'd stopped? . . . I wouldn't lie, he'd find out. . . . I thought he was goin' after them and get shot. . . . He'd go to Enoch first. . . . He won't get rid of Moses. . . . He'll go back and lay the teachers out.*

Every night Anson made the rounds from bedroom to bedroom. If the day had ended well David, half-asleep, would roll over and split his eye-lids with a fraction of a smile, then flop back on his stomach, bury his head in the pillow, and be asleep before his father latched the door. Jonathan's cautious world required more time to make a dream. He would find a star, a leaf dappled with silver, dancing in the night breeze, a moonbeam caught in the vine that overran his window, and he'd study them for their mystery before he moved his world back to the warm protecting walls of his room. Then he would listen for the latch to click in its socket before he closed his eyes.

Ruth held her world close about her. She pulled her favorite scrap of blanket up to her chin, reached one arm up to wrap around her father's neck, and she was secure until the rattling of stove lids in the kitchen announced another day.

When Anson was making his rounds this night, Ruth's arm came from under her blanket and wrapped around his neck as usual. He asked, "Why didn't you and the boys tell me before?"

"We was gonna, but Jonathan said the only way you could stop it would be to get rid of Moses. You'll never get rid of Moses, will you?"

"Moses will be with us always. And that spotted calf belongs to you."

6

"They're happy children," Enoch said a few days later as he and Anson talked. "Children understand more than we do sometimes. They're willing to pay the price for love. When there's none to buy, that's when it's sad."

When the last corn shocks had given up their golden ears, the corncrib bursting at its seams and the fodder piled in giant hutches for cotton-tail rabbits and field mice to enjoy before they were torn down and thrown to the cattle bundle by bundle, there was time for Enoch's settin' and time to help a boy find the right forked sapling for a perfect gravel-shooter.

Enoch hated to see winter come, he always said, because the loafers moved in from the porch and he had to listen day after day to what was wrong with the world and how to fix it. But with night coming early, he could close the store and come and set with Anson and Moses.

Barn chores were started earlier and finished by lantern light, but that still left a gap of time between the end of chores and supper.

Anson could stand in the barn door and drink in the smell of warm animals, June in a December haymow, and horse collars and harness made pungent by sweat soaked up from a plough-horse turning the earth up to the sun.

And with time left over to spend in the kitchen, Moses directed the shaving down of gravel-shooters, cutting the right notches and shaping an old shoe tongue for the sling. There was time to make more whistles too.

Anson didn't say anything, but he thought, if a boy had the best gravel-shooter in school, and whistles to trade, he couldn't be too unpopular. David was a skillful trader and had three jackknives rattling in his pocket before the winter was half over. Jonathan never seemed to accumulate a surplus. Anson decided he probably used his stuff to buy protection.

Ruth felt left out with Moses whittling everything for the boys. But David said, "There's nothing to whittle for girls."

Moses brought a rough board down from the hayloft and asked if he could use it. Anson thought he could find something much smoother, and started to look, but Moses said this was exactly what he needed.

For many nights, before he came in to supper, Moses

worked on something at the workbench in the woodshed by lantern light. Anson told him it was too cold, but Moses kept at it. One night when he came to supper he brought Ruth a doll cradle. It was made of chestnut wood, so smooth Ruth couldn't stop rubbing her fingers over it. There wasn't a nail in it. All the joints were dove-tailed and glued together. Ruth was already convinced that Moses knew everything; now she was sure he could do anything.

After supper, when studying was over, Ruth rocked her doll in front of the fire and Moses talked about chestnut trees.

"You know, there are no more living chestnut trees. They were all killed by a tree fungus from eastern Asia, probably brought to America on an ornamental shrub. Traveling on the wind, it moved over the forests, and neighbor said to neighbor, 'The chestnuts are dying.' Soon there were bare spots in the forest.

"The chestnut was there when the pioneers tamed the wilderness. They built their cabins of it. They fenced their fields with rails quartered from the top-logs, too small for cabin timbers. Ships and wharves were made of its giant lengths. And when the railroads crossed the land, they were built on chestnut railroad ties.

"Frost, or a boy's boot heel, could crack the chestnut burr in half, and there would be brown nuts to eat in autumn. No boy from mid-October to Christmas was without a pocket full. When evening chores were done, they were laid on top of the stove to roast. Sometimes maybe a worm would crawl out and squirm a death-dance on the hot lid."

"I'll keep my chestnut cradle forever," Ruth said. She ran her fingers along the edge of the velvety wood.

One evening Moses said, "Tomorrow is the shortest day of the year. I'll hurry from school and we'll go get the Christmas tree. You know why we have to get the Christmas tree tomorrow?"

David said he thought it didn't make any difference what day they went.

"But it does," said Moses.

"Thousands of years ago, before there were calendars, men didn't know much about the world around them. They got very worried when the days began to get shorter, and the flowers died and the trees became bare, and the earth turned brown. They thought the sun and the earth were dying. So on the shortest day they'd find something that was still green and alive, like we find laurel or holly or branches from evergreen trees. And they would pray and touch the earth with the green, begging the earth to come back to life.

"And to bring the sun back to life at the same time, the priests and wise men would build great fires on the hill-tops to warm the sky and drive away the evil spirits of cold and darkness who were putting out the sun.

"So that's why we have to get the Christmas tree to-morrow. And we'll cut a log for the fireplace big enough to burn for a whole day. Then the sun will start coming back to life and the days will get longer. The earth will stop dying too. And after the seed catalogue comes, your father will plant dried-up brown seeds, and green plants will spring up. All because we gather greens on the darkest day of the year to show our belief that there will be a brighter day."

David thought it would have been much simpler for ancient men to have just hurried up with the invention of the calendar.

"But will the earth ever die?" Jonathan asked.

"No, silly—"and Moses was very grateful to Ruth for her quick answer. "There are enough evergreen trees and laurel in all the woods to cut for a thousand years."

Anson Stone listened, remembering the bleak winter before Moses Waters had come into their lives, knowing that indeed the earth had been brought back to life.

So the winter passed. Moses didn't lose many of his scholars when cold weather came. When the crops were in and the pulpwood chopping slackened, Duncan and Devon Sherman and two of Zeb Long's boys en-rolled. Duncan Sherman quit his job with Rube Flint, the county's biggest land-owner, to enroll, when he heard about the teacher from his younger brother. Rube needed him for feed-lot work, and sent him word to come back. But Duncan didn't go.

In the store, Enoch heard the Lawhorns laughing to their friends that "Rube was awful mad." Rube and the Lawhorns were in-laws. According to the Lawhorns, Rube had said, "I'm gonna git my nigger back if I have to burn the god-damn school and shoot that uppity, edi-cated nigger that teaches it." Enoch told Anson that he didn't see how doing Rube's feed-lot work would be much of a job. His cattle, with ribs and hip bones sticking through their hides, didn't look like he let go of much feed.

Duncan Sherman was sixteen years old. He'd worked for Rube for two years and got $15.00 a month; ate his meals on the back porch in the summer, in the smoke house in the winter, and slept in the loft of the granary year round. He stayed in school with Moses for the rest of the year. "Stay in school," Enoch had said to Duncan, "and I'll give you work next summer at the going wage."

Anson was worried. "They'll do something," he told Enoch. "You know how those Lawhorns hold a grudge."

Moses taught David and Jonathan to use an ax, so Anson bought a light-weight one for each. One evening as he and Moses passed the wood-pile they noticed a length of wood left on the chopping block and Jonathan's ax beside it.

"It isn't like him to leave his tools out," Moses said

as he picked up the ax, ran his finger along the edge, and stood it inside the wood-shed door.

In the kitchen Jonathan sat on a low stool with his books spread out on a chair bottom for a desk.

"You're too far from the light," his father said.

Jonathan turned a pale face up to his father, his eyes filled with a mixture of pain and guilt. The two men saw it at the same time—a thin stream of red, no wider than a pencil, pushing its bulbous front along the center of the floor board from under the chair.

"You told me not to use it except when Moses was there. I cut my new school shoes too."

By now Moses had lifted Jonathan gently over the chair and moved to the light. Up across the arch ran a long cut—through laces, eyelets, tongue and sock. David stood watching behind the stove, pale and quiet. Ruth went to Jonathan's side and took his hand, saying as she did, "Can I ride to the doctor's too? Jonathan gets hurt enough for all of us."

"Everybody's got to have their own peck of troubles," Mrs. Connors volunteered. She began to mop the floor.

It was very late when they got Jonathan back from the doctor's and tucked into bed. Ruth and David had been sent to bed by Mrs. Connors, but had managed to stay awake. Ruth asked, "Did it hurt?" And David, with an element of envy in his voice, said, "Are you gonna miss more'n one day of school?"

Anson and Moses were eating the supper that Mrs. Connors had left in the warming-closet on the back of the stove when a knock came at the back door. Anson opened it and looked straight into the eyes of Mort Lawhorn, the oldest of the five Lawhorn brothers who lived, according to Enoch Morris, "by bootlegging and bullying."

Whoever spoke out to the law against them usually had his barn catch fire mysteriously, the tires cut off his car, or, as in the case of Jake Cummins, suffered a much worse fate.

The Lawhorns had moved a line fence between their property and Jake's in order to get a spring in their own pasture. Jake took them to court and won the case. A few months later someone beat Jake into unconsciousness and threw him into his own hog-pen. Before he was discovered, the hogs had mangled an arm and leg so severely that Jake would walk with a bad limp, swinging a stiff arm, the rest of his life.

"I run outa gas. Got a little you can lend me?" Mort asked.

Anson walked to the truck shed and gave Mort a gas-can, saying as he did, "You can just leave the empty can by the gate. I'll pick it up in the morning."

"I'm much obliged," the tall leader of the Lawhorn clan said as he walked toward the gate.

Anson Stone wondered what they were doing on this

road at this time of night. There were only Hillyer's and Reynolds' farms besides Moses' cottage, and then the road came to a dead end. The whole Lawhorn tribe lived beyond Cedar Corners, in the Green Hill section, and considered it their community service "to keep the niggers of Cedar Corners in line." This they accomplished by terror and fear.

"I wonder what the Lawhorns are doing on our road," Anson said to Moses when he was back in the kitchen. "Neither Hillyer nor Reynolds ever has any dealings with them."

The two men heard the truck cough and rattle off into the night. Moses had remained silent as Anson talked.

"I must be getting up the hill," he said at last. "It's late."

Outside, the two men stood for a long time at the door-yard gate. A fraction of moon showed through a split in the clouds that drifted over the winter sky. For a long moment Anson Stone felt a cold loneliness creeping over him. Then the black man soaked it up with his soft voice as he lifted the gate latch: "I'm glad the cut wasn't any worse. I think I'll shorten the handle before he chops again."

From the gate, Moses took the path that would lead past the barn to the fields rather than to the road, saying, "The clouds have passed the moon now, so I'll go home through the fields."

Anson started to say "It's longer by the fields," but didn't. Moses didn't want to meet the Lawhorns on the road.

Anson studied the sky as he turned toward the house. The dark will overtake him before he's home, he thought. More winter clouds were rolling toward the moon.

The next morning Anson Stone had just come down the stairs when he heard a faint knock at the kitchen door. Moses Waters stood there.

"I didn't sleep much last night," he said. "I stumbled over something on my porch, and when I opened the door and lit the lamp, what do you think it was? One of Duncan and Devon Sherman's fox-hounds. Shot through the head."

"Think it might have been done accidentally by the boys hunting, and crawled there to die?"

"No, shot close up. Right between the eyes with a shotgun blast. No blood around, so it was done somewhere else and brought there."

"Those boys loved their two fox-hounds." Anson concealed his anger. "Identically matched pair."

"I guess it's the Lawhorns' way of telling me that Duncan better go back to work for Rube," Moses said.

Anson was thinking. "There are varmints and varmints. The ones that eat a cabbage plant or nip the buds off peach trees can be fenced out. The ones that molest, bully, torment, and sometimes destroy cannot be fenced out. They enter by the gate and door that a man has built in the simple belief that others will treat him the way they would like to be treated."

"I hope no harm comes to Duncan," the black man said.

"We'll have to see. I'm glad you weren't there when they came."

"They'll be back, I suppose," Moses said as he buttoned his coat and prepared to leave.

"Tell Duncan not to say anything to anybody. We'll just have to wait."

Days passed. Enoch and Anson talked a lot and waited. Nothing happened. Moses Waters kept his certain pace through the earth. He went home at night by the road. Several times he stayed late at Cedar Corners to help when there was sickness and walked home late at night. It worried Anson. The Lawhorns, not seen much in daylight, took great pride in the fact that their friends called them "the night-riders."

Moses had been the lone figure in the church balcony from the first Sunday that Ruth had waved and smiled at him. But since then Reverend Gordon had improved as a man in the eyes of Anson Stone. He had taken to asking Moses to lead the congregation in prayer.

The black man would move noiselessly down the steps, bow his gray head, fold his black hands in front of him, thank his Maker for all His blessings. He never asked for rain if there was drought, or bountiful crops at planting time, as Reverend Gordon did. Then he moved as silently back up the steps as he had come down.

"They couldn't scare him," Enoch said one day. "He's licked 'em. Have you ever noticed that when he prays in church he begins every prayer with 'Hear me when I call, O God.' Strange thing, I happened across it the other night when I was leafing through the Bible. It's the beginning of the Fourth Psalm. And here's how it ends. Wait, I've got a Bible right here in the back room."

Anson followed Enoch to the back of the store. Enoch opened the Bible and read aloud:

I will both lay me down in peace and sleep: for thou, Lord, only makest me dwell in safety.

"I watched him Sunday when he walked back up and I decided right then and there—he believes it."

On the way home Anson wondered if God could do anything about the Lawhorns.

Hearing the winsome call of a bluebird, he looked up and saw it tracing an April symbol across the late February sky, flying toward his orchard. It was time to look at the fields. It was a rule he followed year after year: The day he saw his first bluebird, he went to stand at the bar-way on the highest point of his land to look at the fields.

Just when he got home, Ranger rounded the house with the new collie pup that had arrived at Christmas. Moses had said they had better not wait 'til summer if they wanted a pup to grow up with Ranger's habits, for Ranger was showing his age more and more as winter drew on.

But age and change in length of days never confused the old dog as to when he should start for the school bus. Ranger turned his graying nose up to Anson at the gate, growled at the pup who was pestering him to play, and started down to meet the children.

"Moses will be along soon," Anson mused to himself. "I'll wait for him."

"I saw my first bluebird today," he said when Moses came. "The days are getting longer. Let's walk up and look at the fields we haven't seen all winter."

So they went up together to find that spot of earth in the fields that stirs and holds a man more than any other. A spot of earth where life is remembering, and life is time running a beautiful race. Here a man dreams of the warm, dark earth, turned up to soft April rain and sun. Here the lowering dusk of February does not blur the vision of deep furrows, long rows of tall corn, the undulating waves of golden grain swinging to the rhythm of the eternal theme of nature's constancy. Here, in this spot, the cold wind, the frozen wagon ruts, and the effortless, low slanted rays of the sun lose their meaning and winter's dark lifelessness disappears. At the gateway to his high meadows there comes to a man from his fields, and settles deep within him, the vast, primeval hope of spring and resurrection.

When spring came and the children raced a warmer breeze through the orchard, Ranger growled his jealousy of the young dog who followed, and resigned himself to standing on his stiff legs, watching, lifting an ear to listen if laughter turned to angry shouts. But age could not stop him when he was needed to protect his own.

One day at lambing time a young ewe came in with the flock, leading a new lamb. Everything seemed normal enough to Anson and Moses as they filled the hay-rack and started for the house. But Ranger was disturbed. Something in the orchard drew him up the hill. He circled a spot, then started down, then went back again. His short, aged bark convinced Moses that he should go up.

There, fallen into a woodchuck hole, was a lamb. The ewe had had twins and, unable to keep them together and afraid to stay behind when the rest of the flock came in, had settled for one. When Moses folded the ball of soft fleece in his hands, Ranger managed a feeble wag of his tail. Anson noticed that Moses slackened his pace so that the man and the dog came down the hill together.

"I don't think there'll ever be another dog like Ranger," Anson said.

Once on a cold winter's night, when one of the few snows of the year had fallen, Ranger had whined and scratched at the door. When Anson opened the door, thinking the doghouse had gotten too cold for him, Ranger raced off into the night, barking as he went. After he had done the same thing a second time, Anson lit the lantern and followed him to the barn. One or two ewes with lambs fed at the rack in the shed. The others milled around the outside rack. Ranger darted in and out among them. Here and there the snow was strewn with hay, but Anson could find nothing out of the ordinary.

As Anson came back to the house, Ranger circled him, barking and running back toward the lot. Anson went a second time, looked again, walked through the barn. Some wild animal came around, he thought. At the door he gave Ranger a stern command to quiet down, and the dog, as always, obeyed him.

The next morning a new-born lamb lay frozen in the snow, white as the snow itself. Ranger had raced ahead and beckoned with his bark. Anson noticed the imprint of a dog's body with front paws outstretched in the snow. Ranger must have lain through the night with the dead lamb between his paws, trying to lick it back to life.

Ranger could not stand to see anything or anybody hurt. He would harass and pester a woodchuck out of the garden, but never kill it. If Anson scolded a child, Ranger would take his place between father and child. If

child and dog played together at the edge of the lime-
stone precipice that the brook had been cutting away for
a thousand years, the dog was always at the edge in front
of the child. If a stranger came, he took his place between the stranger and those he owned and loved.

When dogs die, they will crawl under buildings, into
crevices and caves, to die alone and out of sight; even
when run down in the streets or on the highways, they
will try to pull themselves into a storm sewer or culvert.
Sometimes a hunter grown old and crippled, or a farm
dog no longer able to bring the cows, will just not be
around one morning. He will have hidden himself so
well to die that never a trace is found.

That summer Ranger died, as nobly as he could. He
was denied the dog's natural preference for choosing
his place to die, because he was paralyzed. Having
grown slower and slower, and his black nose turned
gray, he gave up trying to meet the school bus and would
wait at the gate.

Time rapidly drew in the circle wherein Ranger had
lived his pleasant life. One morning he dragged himself from his doghouse—his hind legs and half his
body paralyzed—and all day he lay in the sun by the side
of the house. When the people he had owned so long
passed, he could no longer wag his tail; but he followed
them with his mellow, accepting eyes. Anson thought to
move him. But Moses said, "He has always liked that

spot. His coat is thick, so lying on the flat stones is not uncomfortable." By evening Ranger could not move his front paws. So the infrequent struggles to rise also ceased.

Only the eyes and the voice remained. The eyes were resigned, but the voice showed its resentment for time's closing circle. It broke out of the closing circle and went back and back.

The bark was no longer the deep, tired, slow bark of an old dog. It was the bark of a young dog. It came at intervals through the night. Now it was the nervous alternating whine and clipped bark of a frightened pup. It became the confident yelp of a proud young driver with thirty ewes moved into the lot and through the gate. And now it was the sharp forceful voice saying, "I'm standing between the child and you, whoever you are." Now it was the repeated warning, the call of danger—"Come quickly, Ruth is standing on the edge of the bank that overhangs the water-hole." "Jonathan is crying." "The calves are in the garden." "David is on top of the highest beam in the hay-loft." Now it was the cheerful whine and yelp at the door-yard—the black man has just walked into the yard.

Wherever the circumference of his time had reached, the young Ranger raced out the night's gentle delirium of memory. The path through the orchard, along the stream, into the fields, past the gate, down the road to the school bus, leaping up on the door-yard gate, searching a lost lamb. Denying the chance to crawl away to a dark entrance, denying the dignity of aloneness and a will for removing death from the location of life, the circle continued to close. In the morning it was a spot, a spot on the stone walk by the side of the house. The spot where the old dog had died.

Jonathan said, "Let's bury him near the sycamore in the pie-shaped pasture. From there he can look down and see the sheep and cows grazing the pasture and the orchard." And Ruth broke a lilac sprig from along the cemetery fence and put it on Ranger's grave.

When Moses came to work the next morning, he carried a brown paper bag.

"What's in the bag?" Ruth asked when she could stand the suspense no longer. For after the doll cradle there had been neatly carved doll chairs and tables, and once a doll broom, all usually handed to her in a brown paper bag.

"A rose for Ranger's grave," the black man said. He had long since planted the rose slips Enoch had rooted for him. And had rooted many of his own. "You and the boys go and plant it when the dew has dried off. I had a dog to love once."

"What was his name?" Jonathan asked.

"Sounder," Moses answered, and added, "he was a hunting dog and had a beautiful voice."

7

TIME, running its beautiful race with Ruth, Jonathan, and David Stone, moving too slowly for them— "I'm nine going on ten." "I'll be twelve next year."— carried Anson Stone and Moses Waters along with it too fast. From sun-up to sundown, time ran into the Sabbath and rest. Spring ran into the fullness of harvest, and then the earth rested. Fires of hope, kindled on the highest hills of hearts by ancient priests of dreams, re-lit the sun to measure the years.

Every second spring Moses Waters gave his dooryard fence and picket gate a new coat of whitewash and trimmed back Enoch's roses so they wouldn't get out of hand. He made brooms during the long winter evenings, and Enoch sold them at his store. He bought a second-hand car that rattled and coughed to and from his Cedar Corners school. Nature's order of colors bloomed by his porch steps—the bright gold of spring, the blue and pink of summer, and the deep red and bronze of autumn. Sometimes when the pace of work slackened he sat propped against a tree and dangled a fishing pole in the brook that ran between Anson's and Enoch's land.

One summer he asked Anson if he could have August off from work. He was going north to spend the whole month with his doctor son. Anson drove him to the bus.

Five days later Anson walked out in the morning, and Moses was standing by the door-yard gate. All he ever said was, "When children grow up they have their own family and interests; they change with the world." The day after he was back, Ruth got a postcard he had mailed to her. She put it away with her treasures and told the boys never to mention it.

If Moses Waters had become a gentle legend walking the earth for Ruth, Jonathan, and David, legend moved toward sainthood in the minds of Enoch Morris and Anson Stone. "An epic life unfound," Enoch said. "In another climate of appreciation, in land not sour beyond sweetening, his epic life would have been found. He makes quality the foundation of his own self-respect, and whatever he does reveals it. Without being aware of it, he does the ordinary thing in an uncommon way. His life is fulfillment because his heart directs itself toward an excellence for everything he touches. He doesn't know that his gentle step sets the cadence for better walking in the earth."

Sometimes Moses talked to Anson and Enoch about his hopes for some of his pupils at Cedar Corners—his scholars, as he always called them.

Duncan Sherman had not gone back to work for Reuben Flint. Instead, he had gone to Philadelphia after he finished Moses' school, become a policeman, and received the city's highest award for bravery. The story had been sent back to the newspaper at the county seat; the mayor of Philadelphia had written the mayor of the town. But the story never appeared in any paper. The mayor of the town never called Moses Waters to the courthouse steps and stood under where the flag hung and said: "Accept this medal for the boy whom you taught that courage, like love, removes forever a price-tag from human life. He remembered your teaching."

Devon Sherman and Orey Long went away to help fight in the war. Devon died overseas. Orey died saving a white man's life in a ship's explosion and fire.

But most of Moses' scholars remained unfound or lost. After the eighth grade, which some of them did twice because there was no school for them to go to after that, they worked on the pulpwood and logging trucks or drifted away to the mills.

Yet Moses always seemed to know where his scholars had gone. Sometimes he would ask Anson for pay in advance and be gone for several days. He never said, but Anson knew. Someone was in jail or some other trouble. When Moses spoke of someone who needed help, he spoke not of an individual, but of "my people."

Moses had coaxed grass to grow on the sour land of the Cedar Corners school yard. He had put beaded pine boards on the ceiling to keep his scholars warm. He accepted vandalism and insult quietly, and only long after some barbaric action would word of it come to Enoch or Anson.

Several times Moses opened the schoolhouse door in the morning to find that someone had thrown a dead skunk inside during the night. Once the stovepipe was stuffed with oil-soaked rags and when he built a fire the school almost burned.

The years made no perceptible change in either Moses Waters' walk or countenance. But Anson more and more often found excuses to say at dinnertime, "I think we'll wait and start this job tomorrow," and then to suggest that Moses go fishing with the boys or tinker at his own place. There were times, also, when the season made the fields too dry or too wet. It gave Anson a good feeling when Moses, with or without the boys, took his fishing pole and started for the brook and the quiet shade of the giant trees that overhung it.

Lost in summer dreams on such a July afternoon, Moses Waters wandered past a flood-gate which Anson had pointed out as the end of his land and the beginning of Reuben Flint's. The brook wound two miles and picked up two others before it left Rube Flint's twelve hundred acres.

Most people shunned both the man and his land with equal care. As brother-in-law to the Lawhorns, the rumor persisted that he "married to get the protection of their guns." *No Trespassing* signs encompassed his whole domain, yet he could be seen at almost any time of day, riding his land with a shotgun across the pommel of his saddle.

He was a bent, cadaverous man with eyes pulled close together as though they suspected each other's glance and wanted to see each other across his nose. With an upper lip too narrow, his teeth showed as though he were perpetually snarling. Perhaps it was this that caused him to speak in a high-pitched, hissing, whisper-like voice that carried farther and seemed louder than an average speaking voice. Enoch Morris said it was not Rube's narrow lip that affected his speech, but that "he'd strained his vocal chords cursing his wife, his hired men, his sheep and cattle, and every other living thing in God's creation."

This was the voice that shook Moses Waters from his reverie with the question, "What are you doing on my land?"

Moses turned to find the gaunt, pinch-faced man staring down at him, the ever-present shotgun balancing in the bend of his elbow. Several feet away his raw-boned roan horse stood by the fence.

Moses opened his mouth to speak, but Reuben Flint added Moses to the long list of those he abused and cursed. Moses was forced to walk in front of the shotgun to Rube's house. Rube called the sheriff and game warden. While he waited for them to come, he locked Moses in an empty corncrib with two stray dogs he was also holding for the game warden for molesting his sheep.

Moses was amazed at the speed with which the sheriff arrived. Several times when Moses had had Enoch Morris call the sheriff about destruction of his school property, or some injustice to his people, the sheriff had not come at all.

"I work for Mr. Anson Stone; he'll go my bail," Moses said to the sheriff as he was pulled from the corncrib and hand-cuffed.

Later, when the sheriff ordered Moses to climb down from the truck, saying to Anson as he did, "This nigger says he works for you and you'll stand his bail," Anson noticed that not one flicker of fear disrupted the quiet dignity of the black man's eyes.

"I will go his bail," said Anson, "and take those irons off his hands."

In the Justice of the Peace court a few days later, Moses was fined five dollars and court costs for trespassing. The costs came to eighteen dollars and fifty cents. Anson and Moses had been ordered to sit on a backless bench in the middle of the room during the proceedings. Reuben Flint identified the trespasser. When Moses left the court the hissing voice came to him from where Rube sat in an arm chair between the Justice and the sheriff: "Stay off my land."

They walked around the corner of the courthouse where a sign pointed to the Justice of the Peace Court, which was a single room attached to the jail. Moses said, "Justice of the Peace. What a beautiful name for a court. I think it got its name long ago when men fled to the courts to find shelter and asylum from blood-revenge and from the eye-for-an-eye, tooth-for-a-tooth principle practiced in the olden days by barbaric men to satisfy their thirst for vengeance."

"Let's look in at Weinberg's store," Anson said. "I don't need to buy anything, but I like to pass the time of day with Isaac when I'm in town."

"I hope I never have to go to court again," Moses said as they passed down the last step leading from the courthouse yard.

A few weeks after Moses had trespassed on Rube Flint's land, one of the Cedar Corners people came to tell Moses that someone had taken the schoolhouse door off the hinges, chopped it up and piled it in the corner of the schoolhouse with the other fire-wood. All the stovepipe had also been taken down and stomped flat, then each piece bent double.

"The Lawhorns," Enoch said.

Moses smoothed pine boards and built a beautiful new door for his school. He bought a half window and fitted it in the door. "It will give more light in the school-house," he said.

One September evening Moses worked late in the school, putting up new stovepipe and making new backs for some of the school benches that had been knocked off the same night the door was destroyed.

He was almost ready to go home when a truck rattled to a stop in front of the school. He glanced through the glass in his new school door just in time to see two of Mort Lawhorn's boys half push, half throw, Rachel Crawford from the truck. "She fell on her hands and knees in the gravel and stone and they drove on without so much as a glance backward," Moses told Anson Stone late that night.

Rachel Crawford had been one of Moses' best scholars. She was fifteen and had finished his school the year before. She worked with her mother, Theodosia Crawford, at housework: washing, ironing, scrubbing floors in half a dozen houses spread so far apart that "walkin' takes as long as workin'," Theodosia Crawford said.

Moses was always carrying books to lend Rachel. She was bright and ambitious, wanted to be a nurse some day.

Her father, Jesse Crawford, had been buried alive in a landslide when the railroad was cutting the Iron Gate pass. He was left under hundreds of tons of earth and stone. "Too expensive to try to move the fill," the contractor had said. It had hurt Theodosia that he couldn't have a respectable burial. "He always kept up his burial insurance," she said. But as time passed she got over her sorrow and said, "It don't make no difference. When he wades in the Jordan all the Iron Gate mud'll be washed away."

Moses Waters carried Rachel Crawford in his arms the half mile up the road to her cabin. He listened to her sob out her story while her mother washed gravel and earth from her torn knees and shredded palms.

Rachel said she had been walking home when the two Lawhorns had stopped and dragged her into the truck. They had driven into a logging road, where they had molested and beaten her.

The next day Theodosia sent for unlicensed Doc Robinson to come to see Rachel. He was the only doctor she could afford to get to come all the way to Cedar Corners. Most of the doctors liked her people brought to them. Doc Robinson gave Rachel some pain killer and charged her mother three dollars for the visit. That night Moses' bright scholar, who borrowed his books and read so she could be a nurse some day, died.

Theodosia Crawford thought her husband's burial insurance could be used for Rachel, but it couldn't. Moses Waters dug Rachel's grave in the burying ground. No one came from Cedar Corners to help him. He knew his people wanted to, but anything connected with the Lawhorns froze their hearts with fear.

When Ruth came from school she took Moses a jug of fresh water, and David and Jonathan went to help by rolling back the stones that Moses lifted out of the earth.

Three days after Rachel was buried, Moses, Enoch Morris and Anson Stone went to see the County Commonwealth's Attorney. They were kept waiting for a long time in the corridor outside his office. When they were finally admitted Enoch introduced Moses to the young, but rather large, man who kept his seat behind his desk. There were only two chairs in the office besides the one in which the prosecutor sat. He motioned Enoch and Anson to these, but they remained standing with their friend.

Enoch began with his usual blunt frankness. "Two of the Lawhorn boys murdered a child named Rachel Crawford out at Cedar Corners, and we have a witness. Tell your story, Moses."

As Moses went quietly through the details of what he had seen from the window in the schoolhouse door, and the aftermath, Anson studied the face of the law officer. Whether it was a bored grin or a doubting sneer that crossed the prosecutor's face several times while Moses was speaking Anson could not be sure. Whichever it was, it was emphasized by a lack of interest evidenced by the attorney's relaxed jaw that drooped loosely over his shirt collar. The big man's eyes played upon the point of a pencil that he twirled between thumb and fore-finger.

When Moses had finished, the prosecutor pushed his weight further down in the chair and swiveled it in Enoch's direction. He now lifted his eyes and spoke to Enoch, ignoring the man who had told him the story.

"What we have here," he began with a frowned seriousness, "is a darky who says he saw the girl pushed from the truck. Can you see anybody pushed from the cab of a truck unless you're actually in the truck yourself? I've stumbled on, or missed, the running-board many a time getting out of my own car.

"He repeats the story that the girl told her mother. In court this wouldn't be evidence. It would be only hearsay."

Anson watched Enoch shift his weight from one foot to the other. The color had begun to drain from Enoch's face. His lower lip tightened. "All right. What about the doctor?" Enoch asked, acid in his voice.

"Old Doc Robinson would never testify in court."

And the prosecutor began to tap the pencil on the edge of the desk. "It would get him in trouble for practicing medicine with a suspended license. Besides, as you know, he's a morphine peddler, and is even the county coroner illegally. All because he knows the right people."

Enoch's eyes had now become too much for the prosecutor. He went back to watching the pencil, but continued, "What kind of case do you have if the two boys testify that they were just being neighborly? That they were giving the girl a ride home. That she asked to get out at the schoolhouse because she was to meet somebody there. That she was looking toward the school to see if whoever she was to meet was there, and missed the running-board and fell. That she said she wasn't hurt and seemed anxious for them to go on. Maybe they'll be lying but they can imply a lot that might cast suspicion toward the darky here. So much probability. So much circumstance that won't stand up in court."

Enoch shifted his weight again. Anson expected a thunder-clap, but Enoch allowed a long silence to express what all three felt.

Finally the prosecutor dropped his pencil on the desk, spread his hands wide, and looked at the ceiling. "If I think we can establish a case, I'll issue a warrant for the accused."

Enoch opened the door, motioned Moses and Anson out ahead of him. "We have a case. But thank you for your time anyway," he said without looking back, and left the door standing wide open.

"Not at all, not at all; glad to be of service," the prosecutor called after the three departing figures. The only sound that came back to him was the creaking of the floor boards in the courthouse corridor, loosened by a hundred and twenty years of footsteps in search of justice.

As the black man and his friends left the office and crossed the quadrangle between the courthouse and the jail, the sheriff and a deputy glared at them from the steps of the jail. Between his teeth the sheriff muttered profanities. Then he said, "Never misses, six weeks before election and they are trying to stir up a stink. Just question a white man about insulting a nigger just before election, and three-fourths of the county will talk about nothing else. Now I could carry all my votes in my hat. I planned to get most every white vote in that district except them whites who just passed, walking with that nigger. That half-blind idiot who runs the store out there, I never liked him. He's always got his nose in somebody else's business—can't let people alone!"

Off the corner of the quadrangle and out of sight of the sheriff and his deputy, the black man spoke softly to his friends. "Do you think they will arrest the Lawhorns?"

The two white men felt great fear for the safety of their friend if word got out that they had been seen together in the Commonwealth's Attorney's office. But Moses had insisted that he must tell his story himself.

The Commonwealth's Attorney was up for re-election too. He was ambitious. He would not lose votes because one fatherless, destitute child at the far end of the county was dead. He would see that justice was done after election. He just wouldn't have the Lawhorn boys indicted 'til the January court session.

Word got back from the county seat that the black man had told his story to the Commonwealth's Attorney. Enoch picked up snatches of loud laughter and boastful talk about what Moses Waters had to look forward to.

In November, both the sheriff and the Commonwealth's Attorney were re-elected. The grand jury returned an indictment for assault against Mort Lawhorn's two sons. Anson made a trip to the Commonwealth's Attorney to have the court bind the Lawhorns over to keep the peace.

"How could I do that?" the Commonwealth's Attorney asked. "You can't prove that they've threatened anybody."

When Moses' car broke down on the road not long afterwards, someone had shot all the tires full of holes by the time Moses and Anson had finished milking and gone to tow it home.

Enoch and Anson went together to try again to get the Lawhorns bound over by the court.

"That could have been the prank of some of his own school kids," the Commonwealth's Attorney had said. "If you can bring in a witness who'll say he heard these boys threaten harm to Moses Waters if he testifies against them, then I can have them bound over with a peace bond."

"That we will never be able to do," Enoch Morris said as they left. Both men were silent as they walked through the cold wind that whipped around the corner of the courthouse.

The Lawhorns' lawyer got the case moved to the May court session. One of the Lawhorn boys had been stabbed thirteen times with a pocket-knife at a "shootin' match ruckus" by one of the Kecks, and was "still poorly from loss of blood."

And so the winter waned and the sun moved back up the sky. The day Anson saw his first bluebird, he and Moses went to the high land and looked over the fields. The earth was coming back to life.

One morning in April Anson Stone missed the rattle of Moses' car passing on the hard, rutted road. As David left for school his father asked him if he'd heard Moses pass. David said no.

So when Anson had turned the cows and sheep into

the orchard to enjoy the new green that was showing, he walked up to see what had happened to Moses' car this time. It was always breaking down or being contrary about starting.

On the way up the hill Anson drank in the smells and sounds of spring. A great time of year, he thought as he walked. The redbud and dogwood along the fences, and dotting the woods, splashed their red and white against the dozen shades of green, as bright as though they had been washed, over the whole land.

Moses' gate was open. Along his white fence Enoch's roses showed leaves the size of a chipmunk's ear. Following the stones that bordered his walk, daffodils bloomed in straight rows. His peach trees were in bloom. His car stood at the end of the fence where he always left it so he could push it down the hill if it didn't start.

When Anson passed the nearest peach trees, the hum of busy bees came to him. From a tall locust tree at the edge of Moses' land a mockingbird sang impartially to heaven and earth.

The cottage door was open, and Anson, trying to see in, was right upon it before he saw.

Moses Waters lay by the side of his porch steps. Daffodils bloomed there too. His head had crushed three of the flowers against the ground. His gray hair on one side was matted in a brownish-red blotch.

His raincoat hung on a nail by the side of the door. His gum-boots stood together on the floor.

Inside the cottage everything was in order. The tea-
kettle sat on the front lid of the stove. On the table by
the chair, where he read or made brooms at night, there
was an open schoolbook in its brown wrapping-paper
cover. A spool of thread with a threaded needle sticking
in it was beside the book. A shirt was folded over the
arm of the chair.

Along the wall his books stood on their polished pine
shelves: several volumes of *The Nicene Fathers*, a two-
volume set of *Montaigne's Essays*, the *Meditations of
Marcus Aurelius*, the *Writings of Thoreau*, *McGuffey's
Readers*, *The Book of God* by Baruch Spinoza, a book
entitled *Jerusalem* by a man named Moses Mendelssohn,
plus the usual titles—Shakespeare, Burns, Scott—and
three Bibles.

Several glass jars stood by the water bucket on the
shelf that ran under the kitchen window. A white
enameled dipper hung by the side of the window. The
two chairs that Anson and Enoch pulled out when they
came to set on some winter Sunday afternoon were in
their proper place against the wall.

In the sunlight that streamed through the open door
Anson Stone hadn't noticed that the lamp was still lit.
Now he saw it and blew out the light.

*The light. There is a knock at the door. The door
is opened by the man who has been patching his shirt
under the light. He blinks to adjust his eyes to the dark.*

Then everything is dark. The two soft, mysterious, light-like eyes have gone out. A dull thud. The bowl that holds the oil of the lamps is broken and the wicks go down. Everything is dark.

The dull thud. Two cushioned surfaces striking together. Like Ortho Drain wrapping a brick or a stone in a meal sack when he and his boys came to butcher Anson Stone's hogs. Swinging his homemade sling in a wide arc. Looking over the top of the pen at the hog. Striking him right between the eyes. And the hog's four legs fold under it. Not one kick. "If you cut their throat or shoot them, sometimes they kick and break a ham bone," Ortho Drain says. "Then the ham won't cure. This is the easiest of all. The sack muffles the stone, the hair cushions the skull. They don't feel a thing. They don't even hear it."

The easiest of all. Not even hear the splinters of bone pierce and tear the beautiful fabrics of thought. Not hear again the peepers' loud chorus in the peach orchard. Not hear the mockingbird sing to the moon because its song was too long to be used up in the day. Not hear the Seth Thomas clock, with a picture of Father Time holding his scythe to reap the harvest of years, striking the hour and the half-hour from the pine shelf above the stove. Not hear the tea-kettle give rhythm to the slow deliberate speech of three friends talking. Not hear the earth singing with an ear to

*the ground, pressed against three daffodils. And not
hear a black man stand up in court and say . . .*

The sheriff came in his pick-up truck with a deputy.
"Is this still a moonshining place like when old Armentrout lived here?" he asked as he climbed out of the
truck.

He didn't see Enoch's roses. He didn't hear the song
sparrow fuss at him as he leaned over the fence by the
rose bush that belonged to the song sparrow.

"Was this man a heavy drinker?" he asked as he
rolled the body over and crushed more daffodils.

"I've seen him in court before. Never liked a lot of
damn rocks piled along a walk," he said. He stumbled
and kicked a rock out of its straight line. "Busted his
head wide open. Must have fallen all the way from
the door."

"He didn't drink at all," Anson Stone said.

"Well, you oughta know," the sheriff said as he
walked up the steps and entered the cottage.

"Books!" he exclaimed as he stopped inside the door.

The deputy was backing the truck over the garden
where two rows of peas already showed green against
the brown earth. He stopped the truck at the edge of
the porch.

The sheriff came to the door. "Looka here," he said,

with a degree of satisfaction because his investigation was complete, holding a quart jar in his hand. "Quart of moonshine half emptied. No wonder he busted his head."

Anson Stone formed the words "That was planted there," but they would not come out of his mouth. The thought of David when his pony was killed came to him. Grief had closed his lips. Or was it futile to reason in an unreasonable world?

"Who's his family?" the sheriff asked as he screwed the top on the jar and put it on the seat of the truck.

"I'm his family," Anson said. He said that loud and clear.

"I've got to take the body for the coroner to see so there won't be any doubt. You can pick it up in the jail cellar about four o'clock."

The sheriff and his deputy opened the tail-gate of the truck, picked up the body and slid it into the truck the way one would a piece of pulpwood or a fence post. They hooked the tail-gate up and drove away, back over the garden.

Anson Stone looked at the cottage for a long time. Then he closed the door.

Spinoza's *Book of God* would go unread. The white curtains on the windows would turn yellow and fall away to shreds. A wren would build a nest in the sleeve of the raincoat. One of the gum-boots would fall over, and a chipmunk or a field mouse make its home there.

The commotion had driven away the mockingbird and the song sparrow. Anson Stone wondered if they would ever come back. He closed the gate and latched it. The roses Enoch had rooted for Moses Waters would grow wild and one day someone would call them brambles.

Someone would have already told the children at the Cedar Corners school that their teacher would not be coming. Bad news travels on the wind. The last child out would forget to latch the smooth pine door with its glass to see through.

That door would swing back and forth, for no one would ever go to school there again. First the glass would go. Then the hinge that carried the most weight. Then the second hinge. And the door would fall. And one day the roof would fall too, and crash the beaded-pine ceiling to the floor.

Anson Stone walked down the hill. The smells and sounds of spring were gone. The white dogwoods stood like shrouded ghosts. The redbud had turned back to the Judas tree—a name by which people called it because there was a legend that Jesus's cross had been made of its wood. Ever after its bloom was red and shaped like drops of blood.

Moses Waters had said to Jonathan, when he told

him the legend, that he thought redbud was a better name.

Enoch Morris and Anson Stone went with the Negro undertaker to the jail cellar at four o'clock.

Two days later the two white men and four black men from Cedar Corners carried Moses' coffin along the edge of the sexton's garden and up through the burying ground. Reverend Gordon, David, Jonathan, Ruth, and Moses' people from Cedar Corners followed.

The green blades of April bent noiselessly underfoot as they walked, and sprang back into place as they passed. A few dead stalks left over from winter snapped with the crack of burning kindling and lay flat where they were trampled. If catbirds and sparrows still claimed the mock-orange and sword-lily they had decided against a song of protest. When they returned they would never again have to fuss at a whispering scythe, leaving a circle around their nests, for no one would ever come to mow again.

The awful quiet of the brooding earth had poured its heaviness into April's light breeze and made it hard to breathe. It was choking Ruth. So she took her father by the hand and said, "He taught us that the earth sings; he didn't tell us that it weeps."

Up past the sword-lily, the gravestone Ruth had hit with the stone so long ago, close to Anson Stone's pasture, they buried him.

Then deep from the earth you shall speak, from low in the dust your words shall come; your voice shall come from the ground like the voice of a ghost, and your speech shall whisper out of the dust.

ISAIAH 29:4